THE GRAPHIC NOVEL

Wizards of Mickey

1

Contents

Wizards of Mickey
Chapter 1
Walt Disney
The Grand Tournament

IT WAS THE TIME OF LEGENDS, OF WIZARDS AND HEROES...
IT ALL STARTED IN THE PEACEFUL VILLAGE OF MICELAND, AND LIKE ALL GREAT ADVENTURES, IT STARTED WITH SOMETHING VERY SMALL...
...A TURNIP!
FZZZZZ
WELL, NOT THAT SMALL!
SPROING

EEEEK!
THIS ISN'T WHAT I MEANT BY A LARGE HARVEST!
GULP!

B-BACK OFF, OR I'LL USE MY MAGIC TO MASH YOU!

WHAT MAGIC, LITTLE MOUSE?
ZAAAAAP

MAYBE THE MAGIC I FORBADE YOU FROM USING UNTIL YOU'VE COMPLETED YOUR STUDIES AS A SORCERER'S APPRENTICE?
WELL ...

I JUST WANTED TO HELP THE FARMERS. THE LAND'S DRY, THE HARVEST'S POOR, AND...

...AND I SHALL TAKE CARE OF IT, LIKE I ALWAYS HAVE SINCE I MOVED HERE!

WILL YOU USE THE DIAMAGIC, MASTER NEREUS?
YES!

THE MAGIC CRYSTAL CONTROLS THE RAIN. IT HAS ALWAYS SOLVED THE VILLAGE'S PROBLEMS BEFORE, AND IT WILL DO SO AGAIN...

...BUT ONLY AFTER I RETURN FROM THE GREAT LIBRARY OF BUKARA! I HAVE IMPORTANT RESEARCH TO DO.
ZAP
LOOK AFTER THE DIAMAGIC, LITTLE MOUSE!
NEIGH!

WHAT A GREAT SORCERER! WILL I EVER BE LIKE HIM?
CLOP CLOP CLOP

OH! I DON'T BELIEVE MY EYES!

A **MAGICAL STAFF**! YOU MUST BE THE VILLAGE SORCERER.
WELL...

AND THE **CUSTODIAN** OF THE DIAMAGIC!
UMM... Y-YES! BUT... HOW DO YOU KNOW THAT?

THE CRYSTAL THAT CONTROLS THE RAIN IS FAMOUS ALL ACROSS THE LAND!

AND I'M HERE TO...UMM... BORROW IT!
HOLD ON! NOBODY CAN TOUCH THE DIAMAGIC WITHOUT MASTER NEREUS'S PERMISSION, AND HE'S NOT HERE RIGHT NOW.
GREAT! JUST LIKE THE DUKE OF DECEPTION PREDICTED.
I SEE. SO YOU'RE NOT THE REAL SORCERER.
ACTUALLY, I'M...
...A WALKING DISASTER!
PLUTO! WHAT HAPPENED? YOU'RE SOAKING WET!
HEY! YOUR DOG WAS SO BUSY DIGGING UP MOLES, HE KNOCKED OVER TWO BARRELS OF WATER!
WOOF!

AND WE'RE ALREADY SHORT OF WATER FOR THE CROPS! HMPH!
?
SNUFF
SNUFF

I DON'T GET IT. IF YOU'RE THE DIAMAGIC'S CUSTODIAN, **WHY** DON'CHA USE ITS POWER TO HELP THE VILLAGE?

WHO, HIM? **HA-HA!**
LI'L MOUSE COULDN'T EVEN CONJURE UP A **MAGIC PUDDLE**!

FORGET ABOUT USING THE CRYSTAL TO MAKE IT RAIN.
WE NEED THE HELP OF A **REAL** WIZARD!

9

LUCKILY FOR YOU, I AM ONE! THE NAME'S **PETE THE GREAT**! GIMME THE DIAMAGIC, AND I'LL CREATE RAIN.
ZIP

NO WAY! I PROMISED NEREUS I'D TAKE CARE OF IT, SO **NOBODY** TOUCHES IT UNTIL HE COMES BACK.

ALL RIGHT, WHATEVER YOU WANT! IF THE FARMERS AGREE...
BEAT IT, LI'L MOUSE.
LET THE FOREIGN WIZARD TRY!

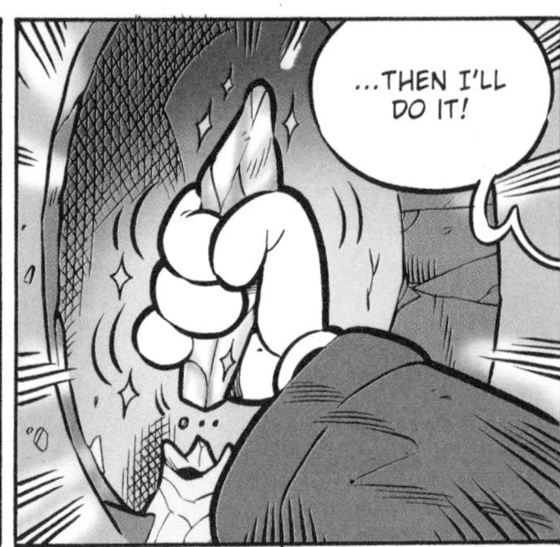

THAT'S WHAT YOU THINK!
LU-RAIN-FOOO!

CRAAACK
SPROOOOSSSh

WOO-HOO! IT'S RAINING!
HOORAY!
HA-HA! IT WORKED!

MAYBE TOO WELL!

CRAAASH

AAAH! A TORNADO!
LI'L MOUSE, WHAT'VE YOU DONE?
OH NO!

MY CHICKENS!
I C-CAN'T STOP IT!
!

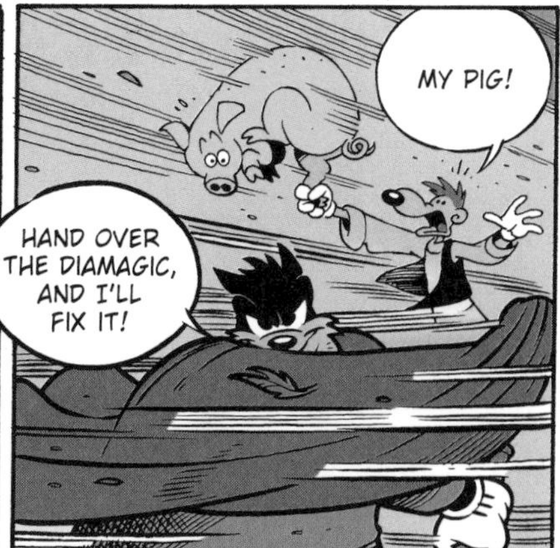
MY PIG!
HAND OVER THE DIAMAGIC, AND I'LL FIX IT!

MY MOTHER-IN-LAW?!
UMM...

WHOOPS! LOST HER.
HERE.

WIND, RELENT! ZAR-WINTAAAR!

THE STORM DRIES UP...
M-MOOOO...
THANKS! WITHOUT YOU, THE VILLAGE WOULD'VE BEEN DESTROYED. I MESSED UP!
YOU JUST NEED SOME PRACTICE, BUDDY.

BUT WITH ANOTHER DIAMAGIC!
FOOOSH

HEY! HOW COME YOUR STAFF ABSORBED IT?

'COS NOW, IT'S **MINE.** WE MADE A DEAL, RIGHT? WHEN I SAID, ***"HAND OVER THE DIAMAGIC, AND I'LL FIX IT"***...

...I MEANT HAND IT OVER ***FOR GOOD! HAR-HAR!***
!

I WON'T LET YOU RUN OFF WITH THE CRYSTAL. I'LL STOP YOU WITH MY MAGIC!
ZAAAP

TSK! HAVEN'T YOU LEARNED YOUR LESSON? YOU'RE ***NOT*** A WIZARD.

YOU'RE NOT EVEN WORTH ***WASTIN'*** A SPELL ON!

SOCK

HAR-HAR! YOU'RE NOT A WIZARD!
A WIZARD? HA-HA!
I FORBADE YOU FROM USING MAGIC!

YOU HAD TO LOOK AFTER THE DIAMAGIC. AND YOU FAILED!

FAILED... FAILED...

SOB! I'M IN THE DOGHOUSE NOW, PLUTO!
WOOF!
THE LITTLE MOUSE DECIDED THE ONLY WAY TO MAKE THINGS RIGHT WAS TO LEAVE THE VILLAGE...

...AND LOOK FOR PETE TO **RETRIEVE** THE DIAMAGIC! HE CROSSED THE FOREST OF MIRE, HAWK PASS, AND THE PLAINS OF SOLITUDE...
...UNTIL HE REACHED GRAND-HAVEN, THE ANCIENT **CAPITAL** OF THE DOLMEN KINGDOM!
POTIONS, MAGICAL MAPS, SCRUMPTIOUS POPCORN!
WOW! I HAD NO IDEA BIG CITIES WERE SO...**BIG**!

WANT A MAGICAL STREET MAP? JUST PICK AN ADDRESS, AND IT'LL TAKE YOU THERE!
HOW ABOUT A PAIR OF SEVEN-LEAGUE SLIPPERS?

LIZARDS FOR POTIONS—THREE FOR THE PRICE OF TWO!
WANNA TASTE OUR SOUP, STRANGER?
!

GURGLE!
HAVE YOU GOT BROCCOLI FOR BRAINS? WHY'D YOU LET A STRANGER TASTE OUR SECRET RECIPE?

URGH! IT'S BITTER...NO... TOO SALTY... BLEAH... AND SO SPICY!

UGH! IT'S THE WORST SOUP I'VE EVER HAD.
BUT HE TURNED GREEN! THAT'S ONE OF THE SPELL'S SIDE EFFECTS.
SLURP
HMM... MUST'VE USED TOO MUCH STINKY ROOT.

SPELL?! THE THREE OF YOU ARE WIZARDS?

OF COURSE! ALMOST EVERYBODY HERE IS.

WE'RE HERE FOR THE QUALIFIERS FOR THE GRAND SORCERERS TOURNAMENT.

HUH? WHAT'S THAT?

HAVEN'T YOU HEARD? SLURP IT'S THE BIG COMPETITION WHERE WIZARDS POOL THEIR DIAMAGIC AS THE STAKES.

WHOEVER SUCCESSFULLY COMPLETES ALL THE CHALLENGES AND CONQUERS ALL THE MAGIC CRYSTALS...

...WILL BE ABLE TO ***UNITE THEM*** TO ***RECREATE*** THE ANCIENT CROWN OF THE SUPREME SORCERER!

I THOUGHT MY VILLAGE'S DIAMAGIC WAS THE ONLY ONE.
HEY! DON'T GOBBLE IT ALL!

WELL, IT'S ALL THE SAME TO ME. I JUST WANNA FIND ***PETE*** AND GET MY RAIN CRYSTAL BACK.
GASP!

I KNOW HE'S HERE IN GRANDHAVEN. DO YOU KNOW HIM?
UNFORTUNATELY, YES! HE'S BEEN PLAYING PRANKS ON THE OTHER WIZARDS SINCE HE ARRIVED. HE'S STAYING AT THE PLUCKED OWL INN...

...BUT YOU'D BETTER ***KEEP AWAY*** FROM HIM AND HIS CRONIES.
I CAN'T!

AND SO...
THE PLUCKED OWL
INN
HAR-HAR! LOOK WHO'S HERE. THE LITTLE GUY WHO THINKS HE'S A WIZARD!

SO FEISTY! ARE YOU HERE TO CHALLENGE ME?
THAT'S RIGHT! I WANT MY DIAMAGIC BACK.

HEAR THAT, BEAGLE BOYS? HE'S CHALLENGING ME FOR THE CRYSTAL!
HUR-HUR-HUR!

TOO BAD DUELS BETWEEN WIZARDS ARE FORBIDDEN 'CEPT DURING THE TOURNAMENT, WHICH I'VE OFFICIALLY SIGNED UP FOR WITH MY TEAM, THE BLACK PHANTOMS.
GRAND
RNAMENT
RULES

SIGN UP, AND MAYBE WE'LL FACE OFF DURING THE QUALIFIERS. WHOOPS, I FORGOT...YOU DON'T HAVE A TEAM!

TOO BAD FOR YOU. WELL THEN... SEE YA! HAR-HAR!
HUR-HUR-HUR!

THE LITTLE MOUSE HAD TO JOIN A TEAM OF WIZARDS. BUT IT WAS TRICKY...
TSK! WHY SHOULD WE TAKE ON A VILLAGE WIZARD?
AGREED. SKEDADDLE, YOU BOOR!

22

SIGH! THAT'S MY TENTH REJECTION IN AN HOUR.

WIZARDS, SIGN UP HERE
THE TOURNAMENT'S GONNA BE OVER BEFORE I EVEN MANAGE TO SIGN UP...

CHEER UP! HAVE A SIP OF MY TONIC.

NO THANKS! I'VE HAD ENOUGH OF YOUR RECIP—ULP!

YOU'RE NOT ONE OF THE WIZARD-COOKS.
COOK? NOPE. A-HYUCK! MY NAME'S GOOFY!

I'M AN *ALCHEMIST* AND A *HERBALIST*!
SWISSS

HEY! THAT SATCHEL'S *ENCHANTED*! SO YOU'RE A WIZARD TOO!
YEAH, BUT DON'T TELL ANYONE.

IN MY FAMILY, EVERYONE'S GOT A PREDETERMINED JOB. MINE WAS WIZARD...

"...BUT I DIDN'T LIKE IT! SO I LEFT TO FIND MY OWN PATH."
A-HYUCK! GOOD-BYE!

BUT... **WHY** DON'T YOU WANT TO USE MAGIC?
I DON'T LIKE USING TRICKS TO SOLVE PROBLEMS...

EEEEK!
WACK! QUICK, HIDE US!

ZOOOW
JUMP IN, **FAFNIR!**
FLUP

A-HYUCK! SO WHO'RE YOU HIDING FROM?

I'M GONNA FIND YOU, YOU **WIZARDING FREELOADER!**

Shush! That innkeeper's gonna pluck this duck!

I BET YOU OWE HIM MONEY.
A TON!
HE LET ME STAY AT HIS INN ON A TAB.
"I PROMISED I'D REPAY HIM BY TURNING HIS SPOONS INTO GOLD...
PREPARE TO BE AMAZED BY THE STUPENDOUS DONALD DUCK!
"...BUT MY SPELL DIDN'T WORK. SOB!"
GRRR!
SEE? NEVER COUNT ON MAGIC TO SOLVE YOUR PROBLEMS.
GROAN! AND MY BABY DRAGON, FAFNIR, MADE THINGS EVEN WORSE.
YARP!

25

"WHEN THE INNKEEPER SAID I'D HAVE TO WASH DISHES FOR THE NEXT SIX MONTHS...
RRR...
"...FAFNIR SET HIS INN ON *FIRE* TO PROTECT ME."
FOOOOOOSH
INN

I'VE BEEN RUNNING FOR TWO DAYS! *SOB* AND I'M ALL OUT OF HIDING PLACES.

YOU SHOULD HIDE IN THE DOLMEN SWAMP! THAT'S WHERE THE QUALIFIERS ARE TAKING PLACE, AND ONLY REGISTERED WIZARDS CAN GET IN.

I ACTUALLY CAME TO GRANDHAVEN TO LOOK FOR A RARE HERB, WHICH ONLY GROWS IN THE SWAMP. BUT THEY WON'T LET ME IN 'COS I'M NOT PART OF A **TEAM**.

HEY, I'VE GOT AN IDEA! WHY DON'T WE FORM **OUR OWN TEAM**?

DONALD CAN **ESCAPE** THE INNKEEPER, GOOFY CAN **FIND** HIS HERB, AND I...

...I'LL HAVE A CHANCE TO **FIX** A MISTAKE!

I'M IN!
ME TOO!

SO...
REMEMBER, YOU DON'T HAVE TO SUBMIT YOUR DIAMAGIC FOR THE QUALIFIERS! YOU ONLY HAVE TO HAND IN YOUR CRYSTAL IF YOU GET THROUGH TO THE TRIALS.

EACH TEAM MUST HAVE A **NAME.** WHAT'S YOURS?

WELL...EVERYONE CALLS ME "LITTLE MOUSE," BUT MY NAME IS MICKEY...

...SO WE'LL BE THE **WIZARDS OF MICKEY!**
WIZARDS OF MICKEY!
HMPH! THE **DUKE OF DECEPTION** WON'T BE HAPPY IF NEREUS'S APPRENTICE JOINS THE TOURNAMENT. I HAVE TO **STOP HIM!**
AND SO, MICKEY, GOOFY AND DONALD JOINED THE GRAND SORCERERS TOURNAMENT! WILL THEY BE ABLE TO PASS THE QUALIFIERS? AND WHO IS THE MYSTERIOUS DUKE OF DECEPTION?
THE END

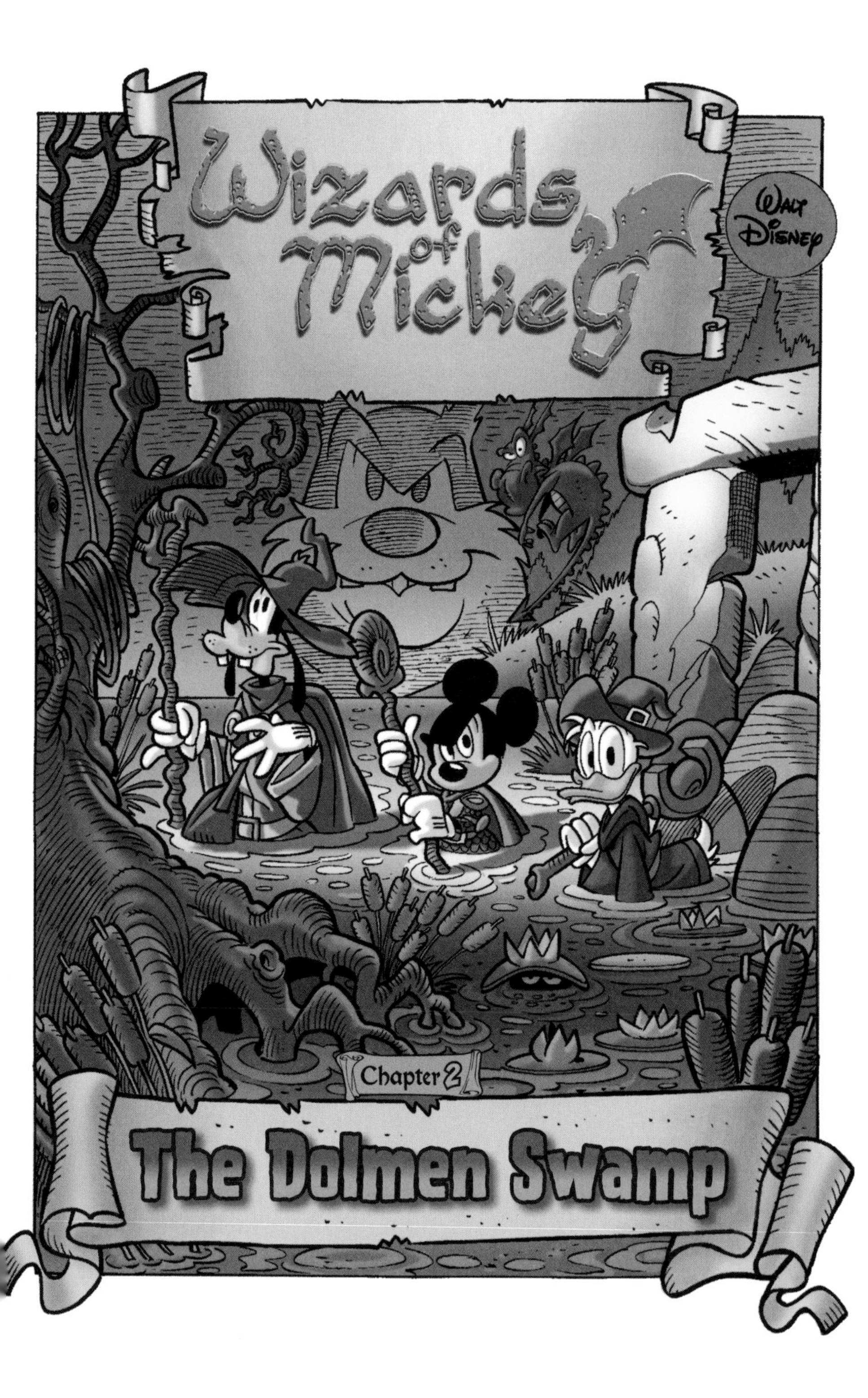
Wizards of Mickey
Walt Disney
Chapter 2
The Dolmen Swamp

IT WAS THE TIME OF LEGENDS, OF WIZARDS AND HEROES...
WIZARDS FROM ALL OVER THE DOLMEN KINGDOM CAME TO THE ANCIENT CAPITAL OF GRANDHAVEN FOR THE **GRAND SORCERERS TOURNAMENT**...
THE RULES ARE FEW BUT STRICT!
TO BE ELIGIBLE FOR THE MAIN TOURNAMENT, YOU MUST RETRIEVE ONE OF THE SCROLLS BEARING THE SORCERER'S ***SEAL*** HIDDEN IN THE DOLMEN SWAMP.

TWO TEAMS AT A TIME WILL ENTER THE SWAMP. THE FIRST TO FIND THE SCROLL WILL QUALIFY FOR THE TOURNAMENT.

ANOTHER RULE—TEAMS MUST CONSIST OF **THREE WIZARDS**. NO MORE, NO LESS!

HUFF! WHY MUST WE ABIDE BY **HUMAN** RULES?
PATIENCE, BROTHER ZAIUS! THE **NO-SCALES** ARE ALWAYS BOSSY.
A-HYUCK!
ZZZ...
HEY, PETE, THERE'S **FOUR** OF US! WHAT DO WE DO?

WE CHEAT! WE'RE THE BLACK PHANTOMS TEAM SERVING THE DUKE OF DECEPTION, RIGHT?

YOU MEAN ONE OF US WILL WEAR THE INVISIBILITY CLOAK AND PARTICIPATE IN SECRET?

THAT'S SO COOL! I WANNA BE THE ONE WHO CHEATS.
CLAP CLAP
CLAP CLAP

SHUT UP! YOU WANT TO GET US BUSTED?
BO-BONK
SHUSH!

THESE ARE THE VILLAINS OF OUR STORY! BUT WHO ARE OUR HEROES?
THERE THEY ARE! HMPH!
YAWN!

LET'S GET TO KNOW THEM!
A-HYUCK! WONDER WHO WE'RE UP AGAINST.
ANY SORCERER'S BETTER THAN THE PEOPLE I NEED TO PAY BACK.

ESPECIALLY THE GUY WHOSE INN FAFNIR ALMOST BURNED TO THE GROUND!
YARP!

WELL, YOU COULD'VE PAID HIM.
HOW? I'M BROKE!

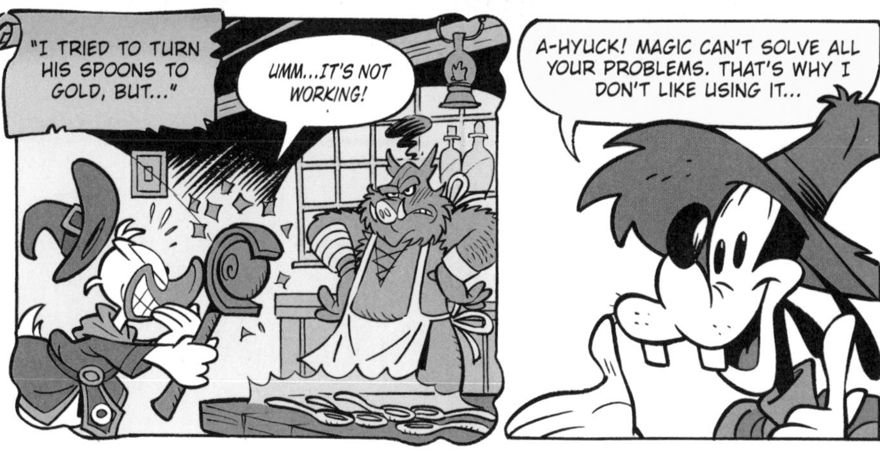
"I TRIED TO TURN HIS SPOONS TO GOLD, BUT..."
UMM...IT'S NOT WORKING!
A-HYUCK! MAGIC CAN'T SOLVE ALL YOUR PROBLEMS. THAT'S WHY I DON'T LIKE USING IT...

...EVEN THOUGH MY FAMILY SAYS I'M DESTINED TO BECOME A GREAT WIZARD.
SWIIISSS

BETTER STICK TO MY HERBAL POTIONS. I CAN'T WAIT TO FIND THAT RARE HERB IN THE DOLMEN SWAMP TO COMPLETE MY **SUPER SYRUP**!

EEP! LOOK OUT, FAFNIR!
I'M GONNA FIND YOU, WIZARD!
LET'S HOPE WE QUALIFY...
PAF

THE TOURNAMENT'S MY ONLY CHANCE TO CHALLENGE PETE...

"...AND GET BACK THE **DIAMAGIC** TO SAVE MY VILLAGE FROM THE DROUGHT!"
HAR-HAR! THE RAIN CRYSTAL'S MINE NOW!

SOB! MASTER NEREUS ENTRUSTED IT TO ME, AND I FAILED HIM. WHAT'S HE GONNA SAY WHEN HE COMES BACK?
BUT NEREUS, IN THE VALLEY OF ANCIENT BONES, ON HIS WAY TO THE GREAT LIBRARY OF BUKARA, HAS BIGGER FISH TO FRY...
ROKNAR! ROKNAR!
WHOOOSHHHH

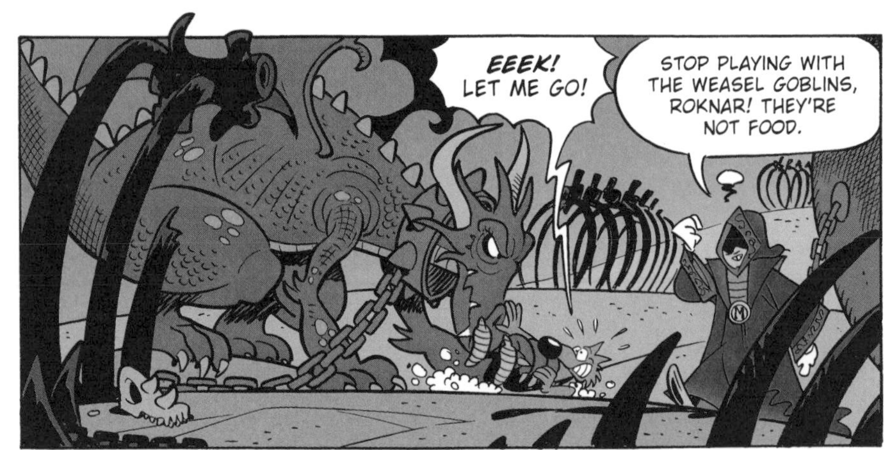
EEEK! LET ME GO!
STOP PLAYING WITH THE WEASEL GOBLINS, ROKNAR! THEY'RE NOT FOOD.

URK... F-FORGIVE ME, MASTER!
IS THE PRISONER IN CHAINS?

A-AS YOU ORDERED!
THEN TAKE ME TO HIM.

LIGHT THE WAY, YOU OVERGROWN LIZARD!
F-FOOOSH
R-RIGHT AWAY, MASTER!

NEREUS, MY OLD FRIEND! YOU FELL INTO MY TRAP!
I KNEW, IF YOU HEARD YOU COULD FIND INFO ABOUT THE DUKE OF DECEPTION IN BUKARA...
"...YOU'D COME RUNNING.
CLOP CLOP CLOP
"TELL ME, DID YOU LIKE THE WELCOME COMMITTEE? HA-HA-HA!"
RAAAWR! GET HIM!

THIS CAGE IS MADE OF THE BONES OF THE ***ANCIENT TITANS!*** THEY RULED THE EARTH WHEN THE WORLD WAS YOUNG AND ONLY DRAGONS KNEW MAGIC.

...THEY'RE **RIGGING** THE QUALIFIERS!
THERE HE IS.

SO, BROTHER, HOW'D IT GO?
I TAMPERED WITH THE OFFICIAL LIST.
VLAP

NOW WE'RE IN THE SECOND ROUND AGAINST A TEAM OF **WIMPY WIZARDS**!
PERFECT. VICTORY WILL BE OURS!

AND THE NEXT DAY...
UGH, I HATE SWAMPS! MY NEW SHOES ARE GONNA GET ALL MUDDY!
FIRST ROUND! THE ***YOUNG MAGIC*** TEAM AGAINST...

...TEAM MAGMA FIRE!
!!!
UMM... WHAT IF WE...?
...GAVE UP?
AGREED!
ZO-OOOOWWWW

TSK! THE NO-SCALES ARE SUCH COWARDS.

WILL YOU DO THE HONORS, BROTHER ZAIUS?

OF COURSE, BROTHER ZEFREN!
TAP
WOOOSH

VLA-AAAAAH

OOOH!
SO POWERFUL!
GET THE SCROLL, ZORON.
FLAP
FLAP
FLAP

PHEW! GOOD THING WE SWITCHED PLACES.
YEAH! WE WERE S'POSED TO FACE THE DRAGONS!

INSTEAD, WE'RE AGAINST THOSE DUDS. HAR-HAR!
WE WIN... THEY WIN...

SECOND ROUND!
BLACK PHANTOMS VS
ENCHANTED FLOWER!
CRACK

BONK
OUCH!

TU-
TU
TUMP
OOH!
AGH!
UGH!

BE QUIET! THE JUDGES
WILL HEAR YOU!

CUT IT OUT, YOU IDIOTS!
WE'RE AT THE WALL OF THORNS...

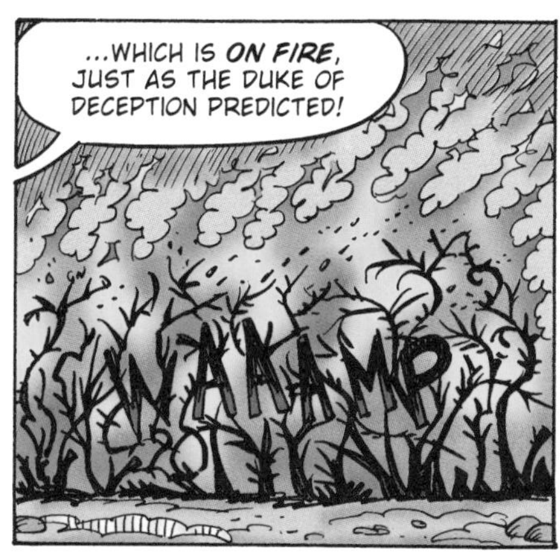
...WHICH IS ON FIRE, JUST AS THE DUKE OF DECEPTION PREDICTED!
WAAAMP

BUT OUR DIAMAGIC'S PERFECT FOR THIS, ISN'T IT?

LU-RAIN-FOOO!

PROOOSC
FFSSSSSSSS

-GASP- PETE'S USING "LU-RAIN-FO," THE RAIN SPELL!

NOW I GET IT! HE STOLE MY VILLAGE'S DIAMAGIC 'COS HE NEEDED IT TO GET INTO THE TOURNAMENT!

THAT'S WHAT **CLASS** LOOKS LIKE.

MISSION ACCOMPLISHED IN JUST SIX MINUTES!

MAYBE THESE **BUMPKINS** THINK THEY CAN DO BETTER!
HEH-HEH!

WE'LL SEE. WE'RE UP!
THIRD ROUND! **WIZARDS OF MICKEY** VS **ALTERUS BAND!**

TSK! THESE CLOWNS BROUGHT A **DOG**...
IT'S NOT EVEN A PEDIGREE!
RRR...

HEY! THIS HEDGE IS BLOCKING THE WAY.
IT GOES ON FOREVER!

AND IT'S ROCK-HARD! IT'S IMPOSSIBLE TO GO THROUGH IT.
TOC TOC

NOT WITH A DIAMAGIC THAT LETS YOU PASS THROUGH LIKE AIR!
ZAN-FRA-LUUUN!

FAREWELL, PEASANTS!

SOB!
I'M ON IT! I'LL MAKE THE LEAVES WILT SO WE CAN SNEAK BETWEEN THE BRANCHES.

HERBIS SHRIVELLIS!
ZAAAP

UMM...NOTHING HAPPENED.
TOC TOC

WACK! HOW COME MY SPELLS NEVER WORK? ARGH!

IF WE CAN'T FIND A ROUTE THROUGH, YOU'LL NEVER ROOT OUT YOUR MAGICAL HERB.
ROOT OUT? A-HYUCK! I GOT IT!

WHILE GATHERING PLANTS FOR MY POTIONS, I LEARNED THAT EVEN THE STRONGEST TREE WILL FALL IF YOU BREAK ITS ROOTS.
SWIIIISSS

THAT'S RIGHT! GET CHOPPING!
ZAP
ZAP
ZAP
ZAP
ZAP

SO...
SFRUSH
FRUSH
PANT! PANT!
HEH-HEH! SOMETIMES, BEING A **BUMPKIN** COMES IN HANDY!
SFRASH
FRUSH
!

THERE'S ANOTHER THING I LEARNED IN MY VILLAGE...

ANIMALS HAVE A GREAT SENSE OF SMELL! RIGHT, DONALD?
TRUE! MY FAFNIR JUST NEEDS TO **TAKE A SNIFF** OF ANY PIECE OF PARCHMENT...

...TO **FIND** THE SCROLL WE'RE LOOKING FOR!
SNIFF SNIFF

ZOOOOWW

QUICK, LET'S FOLLOW HIM!

IN THE MEANTIME, NEREUS'S MEDALLION IS ON ITS WAY TO MICKEY...
SPLASH

CROAK!

ZOMP
ZOMP
ZOMP
ZOMP

UNTIL...
WHOOPS! I ALMOST STEPPED ON YOU.
CROAK!
SPLASH

HEY...THIS IS MASTER NEREUS'S MEDALLION! HOW...?
HURRY! FAFNIR'S TRACKED IT DOWN!

LOOK! THE SCROLL!
YEAH! BUT... HOW DO WE GET TO IT?

THIS BLADE OF GRASS WON'T SUPPORT OUR WEIGHT.

THEN WE'LL BECOME AS LIGHT AS AIR!
?

VICTORY'S OURS, CLOWNS!
HMM...
GRR! THEY FOLLOWED US!

THERE'S SOMETHING ODD ABOUT THAT SCROLL. AS IF...

OF COURSE! I GET IT!

LOOK ALONG THE EDGE OF THE PRECIPICE! THAT'S WHERE WE'LL FIND THE SCROLL.
HUH?
SNIFF
SNIFF

BUT...THE ONE ON THE DOLMEN?

IT'S JUST A **REFLECTION**! HEH-HEH!
!
?

COMPARED WITH THE SCROLL THEY SHOWED US, THAT SEAL...
FRUSH FRUSH

"...IS A MIRROR IMAGE!"

SO THE REAL SCROLL MUST BE CLOSE ENOUGH TO BE REFLECTED. HERE, ALONG THE EDGE!
!
SWISS

NOOO!
CRA-AASH

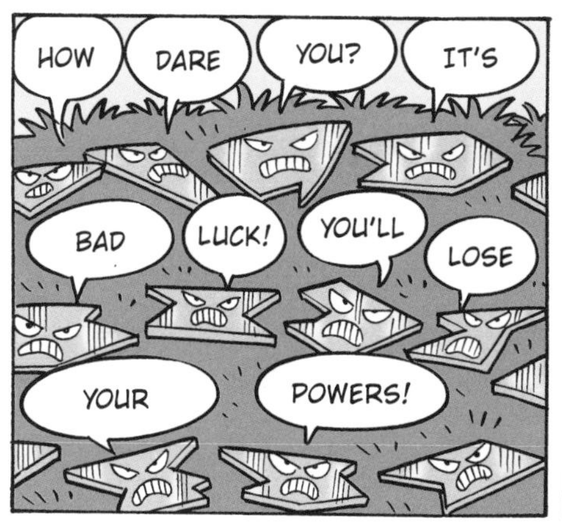
HOW
DARE
YOU?
IT'S
BAD
LUCK!
YOU'LL
LOSE
YOUR
POWERS!

TRUE, BREAKING MIRRORS IS BAD LUCK! HOW'RE THEY GONNA CROSS BACK WITHOUT THEIR POWERS IF THE BRIDGE IS GONE?
?

A-HYUCK! THIS BLADE OF GRASS IS JUST THE HERB I NEEDED FOR MY POTION.
ARGH!
HEH-HEH!
AND SO...
THE WIZARDS OF MICKEY TEAM QUALIFIES FOR THE TOURNAMENT.
PERFECT! NOW... BRING IT ON, PETE!
HOLD ON!
I CHALLENGE YOU! THE WINNER GETS THE DIAMAGIC YOU USED TO CONTROL THE RAIN!

YOU HAVE TO STAKE A DIAMAGIC TOO, MICKEY. HAVE YOU GOT ONE?

WELL...ACTUALLY... NO!

NO DIAMAGIC, **NO** CHALLENGE. THAT'S THE RULE!
I ACCEPT ANYWAY!
...

I ALREADY TOLD YOU. YOU'RE **NOT** A WIZARD...
TLACK

SWIIIISSSH
...AND YOU'RE NOT EVEN WORTH WASTING A SPELL ON!

YOU'RE WRONG! I **AM** A WIZARD...
SWIIISH

HUH? A SEED?
SWIIISH

GREAT MAGIC ALWAYS STARTS...

...FROM SOMETHING VERY SMALL!
!
!
!
!

AARGH! LET ME GO!

I WON! THE DIAMAGIC'S MINE AGAIN!
FoOOSH

THAT'S FAIR! PETE ACCEPTED THE CHALLENGE, SO HE'S MUST PAY THE PRICE.

I DID IT! I CAN BRING THE DIAMAGIC BACK TO MY VILLAGE AND END THE DROUGHT.

AND YOU'RE BOTH INVITED!
A-HYUCK! PERHAPS BEING A HERBALIST ISN'T FOR ME...

...TURNS OUT I'M ALLERGIC TO RARE HERBS!
AND YOUR MASTER CAN TELL ME WHY MY SPELLS NEVER WORK.
GRAT GRAT
GRAT GRAT

POOR DONALD! IF HE HADN'T LEFT IN SUCH A HURRY, HE'D HAVE DISCOVERED THAT...
GOLD! MY SPOONS DID TURN TO GOLD! THE DUCK'S SPELL WORKED...THERE'S JUST A DELAYED REACTION!
24K

MICKEY AND HIS FRIENDS QUALIFIED FOR THE GRAND SORCERERS TOURNAMENT! BUT WHAT IS HIDDEN INSIDE NEREUS'S MEDALLION?
THE END

Wizards of Mickey

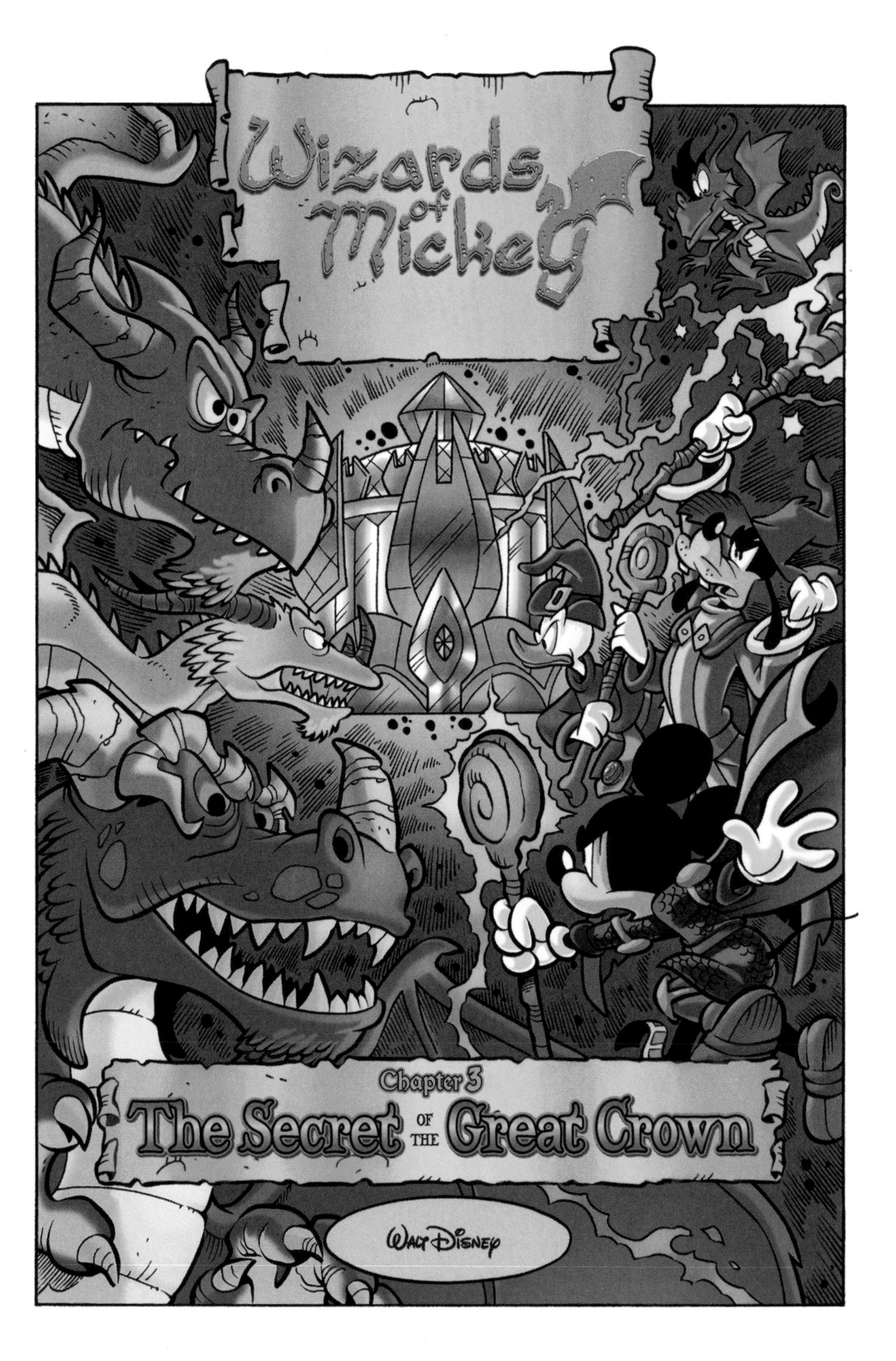
Wizards of Mickey
Chapter 3
The Secret of the Great Crown
Walt Disney

IT WAS THE TIME OF LEGENDS, OF WIZARDS AND HEROES...
AND SPEAKING OF HEROES, MEET THE ONES OF OUR ADVENTURE: THE WIZARDS OF MICKEY!
MICKEY: APPRENTICE SORCERER FROM MICELAND, HE SIGNED UP FOR THE GRAND SORCERERS TOURNAMENT TO SAVE HIS VILLAGE.
GOOFY: HIS FAMILY WANTS HIM TO BECOME A GREAT WIZARD... BUT HE'D RATHER DO SOMETHING ELSE.
DONALD: A VERY UNLUCKY WIZARD. HE CAN ONLY CAST DELAYED-ACTION SPELLS.
FAFNIR: A BABY DRAGON WHO... WELL, YOU'LL FIND OUT SOON ENOUGH!
AND THE BAD GUYS: THE BLACK PHANTOMS TEAM!
BEAGLE BOYS: WIZARDING CHEATERS AND SWINDLERS! THANKS TO THE INVISIBILITY CLOAK, ONE OF THEM IS SECRETLY HELPING DURING THE TOURNAMENT.
WHAT SCOUNDRELS!
PETE: TEAM LEADER AND A POWERFUL SORCERER. HE OFTEN PREFERS HIS MACE TO MAGIC.
AND FINALLY...
THE DUKE OF DECEPTION: HE WANTS TO CONQUER THE WORLD USING THE SUPREME SORCERER'S CROWN. HE COMMANDS THE BLACK PHANTOMS TEAM AND THE WEASEL GOBLINS.
NEREUS: WISE WIZARD AND MICKEY'S MASTER.

IT WAS A FREEZING NIGHT UP ON THE **FROZEN PEAKS**, AND OUR HEROES WERE... FREEZING!
BRRR!
RATTLE, RATTLE!
HMPH! IT'S ALL YOUR FAULT, FAFNIR! WHY'RE YOU ALWAYS SO CLUMSY?
WHINE!
WE COULD'VE TRAVELED COMFORTABLY TO MICELAND WITH CIRCUS PANZUS...
"...BUT YOU RUINED EVERYTHING!"
RAAAA...CHOOO!

RAAAA-CHOO!
CAREFUL! DON'T SNEEZE NEXT TO...
...THE FIREWORKS!
BOOM
OH NO! THE BEARDED LADY'S FAKE BEARDS!
HARUMPH!
THESE POOR STILTS!
SOB! HOW AM I GONNA PLAY THE GIANT DWARF NOW?

SCRAM! AND TAKE THAT FIRE-SPITTING LIZARD WITH YOU!

OOF! AND NOW THAT WE NEED FIRE, YOU HAVE THIS SMOKY COUGH!
COUGH! COUGH!

DON'T SCOLD HIM! SMOKY BRONCHITIS IS A SERIOUS ILLNESS FOR DRAGONS...

...THAT PUTS OUT THEIR INTERNAL "FURNACES"!

IF WE DON'T CURE HIM, HE COULD LOSE HIS ABILITY TO BREATHE FIRE PERMANENTLY.
WHINE!

SOMETHING TELLS ME YOU'VE FOUND A NEW VOCATION. HEH-HEH!

A-HYUCK! FROM NOW ON, I'M GONNA BE A DOCTOR!
MEDICINES FOR DRAGONS AND GIANT TROLLS

WELL, DEAR "DOCTOR," I JUST FOUND A BETTER USE FOR YOUR BOOKS!

AHHH! FINALLY, MY FEATHERS ARE THAWING.

DON'T WORRY ABOUT YOUR BOOKS! YOU CAN ALWAYS TAKE MORE OUT OF YOUR MAGICAL BAG, RIGHT?

WELL, YES...BUT YOU KNOW I DON'T LIKE SOLVING PROBLEMS WITH MAGIC.

THEN DONALD CAN BUY NEW COPIES WHEN WE REACH A TOWN!
WACK!

OOF! MORE DEBTS! I ALREADY OWE MY UNCLE A FORTUNE!

"IF ONLY MY SPELLS WORKED, I'D STILL BE LIVING IN UNCLE SCROOGE'S CASTLE...
I WAS SO SURE THAT POTION WAS GONNA TURN LEAD INTO **GOLD**!
GRRR! WHO'S GONNA PAY FOR THE FLASKS YOU EXPLODED?
KEEP RUNNING! AND DON'T COME BACK UNTIL YOU'VE GOT MONEY!
"AND ON THAT WOEFUL DAY, I ALSO MET...
WHIMPER!
"...MY FIERY LITTLE FAFNIR!"
HMM? ARE YOU CAUGHT IN A SNARE, LITTLE BUDDY?

NNNGH... HERE — YOU'RE FREE! HAPPY, HUH?
YARP! YARP!
FOOSSH
GROAN! GUESS IT'S HIS WAY OF SAYING "THANK YOU."

"FROM THAT MOMENT, HE'S ALWAYS BEEN WITH ME!"
YARP! YARP!

SOMETIMES, I WONDER WHY I LET YOU STAY, YOU SORRY EXCUSE FOR A LIZARD. HMPH!

ROKNAR, DIDN'T YOU SAY YOU ONCE GUARDED THE ***ENTRANCE*** TO THE UNDERGROUND DRAGON KINGDOM?
WELL... YES, MASTER!
TUMP
TUMP

THEN WHY HAVE MY WEASEL GOBLINS BEEN DIGGING WHERE YOU TOLD THEM TO FOR THREE DAYS...

...BUT HAVE YET TO FIND ANY SIGN OF A TUNNEL?!

THE OTHER DRAGONS SEEM TO HAVE SEALED THE ENTRANCE WHEN I ABANDONED MY POST.

THEY CONSIDER ME A TRAITOR FOR HAVING JOINED YOU! GRRR!

WELL, YOU ARE! BUT I LOVE TRAITORS! I'M THE DUKE OF DECEPTION, AFTER ALL.

AND ONCE I STEAL THE SECRETS OF THE DRAGONS' ANCIENT MAGIC, I'LL RULE THE WHOLE WORLD!

PETE! BEAGLE BOYS! I HAVE A JOB FOR YOU.

THERE'S A TEAM OF DRAGON-SORCERERS TAKING PART IN THE TOURNAMENT.

FOLLOW THEM AND FIND THE WAY TO THE CAPITAL OF THEIR HIDDEN KINGDOM!
Gulp Why do we always get the difficult jobs?

MEANWHILE...
FAFNIR, STOP! THIS COUGH SYRUP TASTES AWFUL, BUT IT'LL HELP YOU!
RAAAAR! RAAAR!

GOT YOU!
OOOOF!
TUMP

OH NO!
MASTER NEREUS'S
MEDALLION!

"I STILL DON'T UNDERSTAND WHY A FROG IN THE DOLMEN SWAMP HAD IT..."

AND IT SEEMED TO BE ***LOOKING FOR*** ME, BUT THAT'S RIDICUL— WHOOPS!
TLAC

IT...
IT OPENED!
Ah, Little Mouse! You finally received my *medalophone*.

With this techno-magical item, we shall be able to keep in touch, even though I cannot escape my prison.

PRISON?! WHO CAPTURED YOU, MASTER NEREUS?

The Duke of Deception, unfortunately. Perhaps I should call him by his real name...

...Phantom Blot. We studied magic together!

Y-YOU STUDIED ALONGSIDE THE DUKE OF DECEPTION?

It is a long story... Once, Phantom Blot and I were both apprentices of the Supreme Sorcerer!
BLEAH!

"BUT WHILE I PATIENTLY STUDIED THE **THOUSAND BOOKS OF MAGICAL KNOWLEDGE**, PHANTOM BLOT WANTED TO BECOME POWERFUL QUICKLY...
"THAT IS WHY HE WANTED OUR MASTER'S CROWN, THE **CROWN OF THE SUPREME SORCERER**...
"...WHICH ALLOWS ITS OWNER TO **CONTROL** EVERY KIND OF MAGIC.
"ONE TERRIBLE NIGHT, WHILE OUR MASTER WAS TRAVELING TO ANOTHER DIMENSION...
"...PHANTOM BLOT TRIED TO STEAL THE CROWN!"

"I MANAGED TO STOP HIM, BUT...
"...AS WE FOUGHT, THE CROWN FELL ONTO THE ANVIL OF FATE...
"...AND SHATTERED!
"THE MAGICAL DIAMAGIC CRYSTALS WERE FORMED FROM THE PIECES OF THE CROWN...
"EACH GOVERNS A DIFFERENT MAGICAL POWER. YOU KNOW OF MICELAND'S CRYSTAL..."

...with the power to create rain. But there are many more, sought after by sorcerers.

Only the one who collects all the Diamagic will be able to rebuild the crown and become the *Supreme Sorcerer*!

WE KNOW! THAT'S WHY THEY'RE HOLDING THE GRAND TOURNAMENT!

WE SIGNED UP TOO, AND—*OUCH*!
STOMP

A-hyuck! I don't think Mickey wants his master to know he left the village to join the tournament.
HE COULD'VE JUST SAID SO... OUCH!

MASTER, WHERE ARE YOU? I'LL COME SAVE YOU!
In Bukara, but...

...IT IS A DANGEROUS PLACE, FULL OF GUARDS.
HOW'S THE OLD MAN DOING?
BADLY, I HOPE!

I must go! They mustn't find out we're in contact!

M-MASTER...

A-HYUCK! IT'S JUST LIKE MY GREAT-GREAT GRANDPOPS GOOFUS PHILOSOPHUS USED TO SAY, "PROBLEMS ARE LIKE WAVES—THEY JUST KEEP COMING!"
HUH?
COUGH! COUGH! COUGH!

FAFNIR'S GETTING WORSE. THE COUGH SYRUP DIDN'T WORK!

THEN WE GOTTA TAKE HIM TO SVARTLAND CASTLE.

ACCORDING TO THE TOURNAMENT MAP, THE DRAGON-SORCERERS TEAM IS HEADING THERE...

MAYBE THEY'LL KNOW HOW TO CURE FAFNIR. LET'S GO!

A FEW DAYS LATER, IN SVARTLAND...
OOF! I'M BEAT. MY FEET HURT!

WE'VE BEEN FOLLOWING THOSE DRAGONS FOR THREE DAYS...OUCH... THEY WENT EVERYWHERE BUT HOME.
YEAH! -MUNCH-
DROP THAT SARDINE, YOU THIEF!

WHO, ME? IT'S NOT MY FAULT IF YOUR FISH FLY TO ME!

SEE? HEH-HEH!
SPLAT

BAH! SORCERERS!
HAR-HAR-HAR!

QUIT MESSING AROUND!

THE DUKE OF DECEPTION DIDN'T GIVE US THE INVISIBILITY CLOAK SO WE COULD GOOF OFF!
VLAP!

WE'VE GOT A ***JOB*** TO DO...

...AND I FINALLY FOUND A WAY!
COUGH! COUGH! COUGH!

EXCUSE ME...WE'RE LOOKING FOR THE DRAGONS OF ***TEAM MAGMA FIRE***! HAVE YOU SEEN THEM?

COUGH, COUGH, COUGH!
HEY, THAT SEA BASS DOESN'T NEED TO BE SMOKED!

75

UGH! DRAGONS!
THE DRAGON-SORCERERS ARE IN THE CENTRAL TOWER...

...BUT THEY'RE ONLY GONNA TALK TO CHALLENGERS.
PETE? WHAT'RE YOU DOING HERE?

TSK! I'M TAKING PART IN THE TOURNAMENT! DON'T TELL ME YOU'RE NOT AFTER TEAM MAGMA FIRE'S DIAMAGIC OF SPEED.

HMM...WITH THAT CRYSTAL, I COULD TRAVEL SUPER-FAST. FREEING MASTER NEREUS WOULD BE A PIECE OF CAKE!

C'MON! LET'S GO CHALLENGE THE DRAGONS!
BUT...WHAT ABOUT FAFNIR?

WELL, IF THE DRAGONS ONLY TALK TO THEIR OPPONENTS, CHALLENGING THEM'S THE ONLY WAY TO ASK FOR A CURE!
HEH-HEH! HE FELL FOR IT!

AND SO...WIZARDS OF MICKEY VS TEAM MAGMA FIRE!
TO-ROCK-VAAA! STONE PRISON!
TSK!

IS THIS THE BEST YOU CAN DO, NO-SCALES WIZARD?
WHOA! DUCK!
WACK! WHY DON'T WE ASK FOR THE CURE AND BEAT IT?
WOOSSH

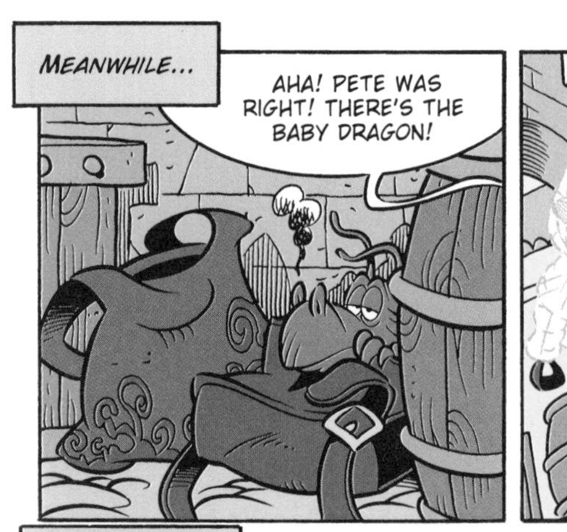
MEANWHILE...
AHA! PETE WAS RIGHT! THERE'S THE BABY DRAGON!

!
IF THE DRAGON-SORCERERS WON'T TAKE US TO THEIR KINGDOM, THEN WE'LL "CONVINCE" THIS LITTLE GUY TO SHOW US THE WAY. HEH-HEH!

AT THE SAME TIME...
RU-GREEN-TOOR! TRAP OF VINES!
HUFF!

URK! THEY'RE GONNA BURN US TO A CRISP!
SPEAKING OF BURNING ...THAT SMOKE'S ***WEIRD***.

IT'S FAFNIR! HE'S SAYING HE'S BEEN KIDNAPPED!

QUICK, MICKEY! WE GOTTA SAVE HIM!

BUT...IF WE ABANDON THE CHALLENGE...
...WE'LL BE DISQUALIFIED. THE DRAGONS WILL WIN BY DEFAULT.

AND I'LL LOSE MY VILLAGE'S DIAMAGIC, WHICH I HAD TO STAKE IN ORDER TO CHALLENGE THEM!

I KNOW, BUT WE CAN'T ABANDON FAFNIR! HE'S A WALKING DISASTER, BUT...

...HE'S ALSO MY FRIEND...

YOU'RE RIGHT! LET'S GO!
HEY! GIVING UP?
THESE NO-SCALES ARE SUCH COWARDS!

A-HYUCK! SORRY TO RUN, BUT WE GOTTA SAVE A BABY DRAGON!

DRAGON? EXPLAIN YOURSELF!
TUMP

AND SOON...
WE SHALL HELP YOU! FOLLOW THE KIDNAPPER. MY BROTHERS AND I WILL CUT HIM OFF!

I DID IT! I GOT THE DRAGON! I GOT THE...

...DRAGON! **EEK!**

WHAT ARE YOU UP TO, YOU RASCALS?

UMM...WE JUST WANTED TO **SEE** A BABY DRAGON UP CLO—OUCH!

GET OUTTA HERE, OR I'LL CAST "**GRE-TANF-PO**," THE SPELL OF **ETERNAL STINK**!
GRRR!

THANKS!
WE COULDN'T HAVE DONE IT WITHOUT YOU.

WELL, YOU SHOWED US THAT NO-SCALES CAN HAVE **NOBLE SPIRITS** TOO...
PSST...

...AND MAKE **SACRIFICES** FOR THEIR FRIENDS.
YARP!

PSST...PSST...
THAT'S WHY WE'VE DECIDED...

...TO DECLARE OUR CHALLENGE A DRAW! YOU WON'T LOSE YOUR DIAMAGIC.

HOORAY!

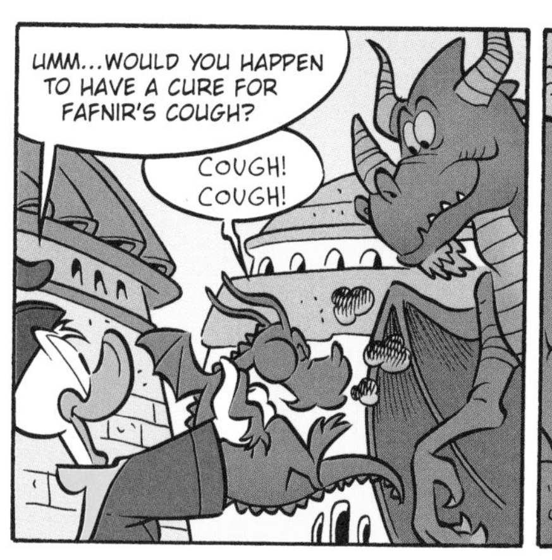
UMM...WOULD YOU HAPPEN TO HAVE A CURE FOR FAFNIR'S COUGH?
COUGH! COUGH!

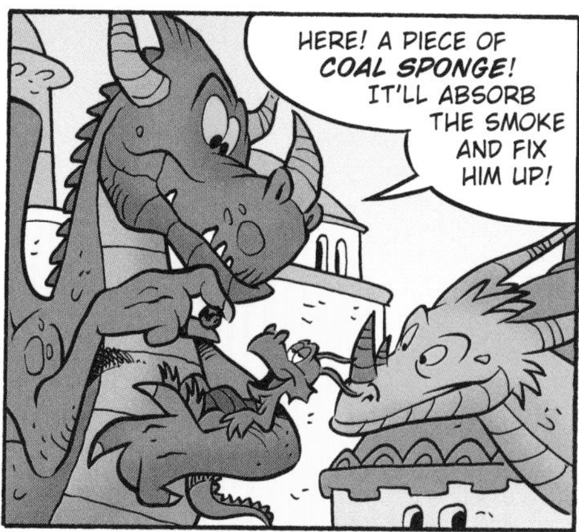
HERE! A PIECE OF **COAL SPONGE!** IT'LL ABSORB THE SMOKE AND FIX HIM UP!

FSSSSS

!
FOOOOSH

GROAN! I KNOW...IT'S HIS WAY OF SAYING, "THANKS!"
HA-HA-HA!
AND THAT WAS HOW THE WIZARDS OF MICKEY BECAME FRIENDS WITH THE DRAGONS! BUT WILL THEY BE ABLE TO SAVE NEREUS?

Wizards of Mickey

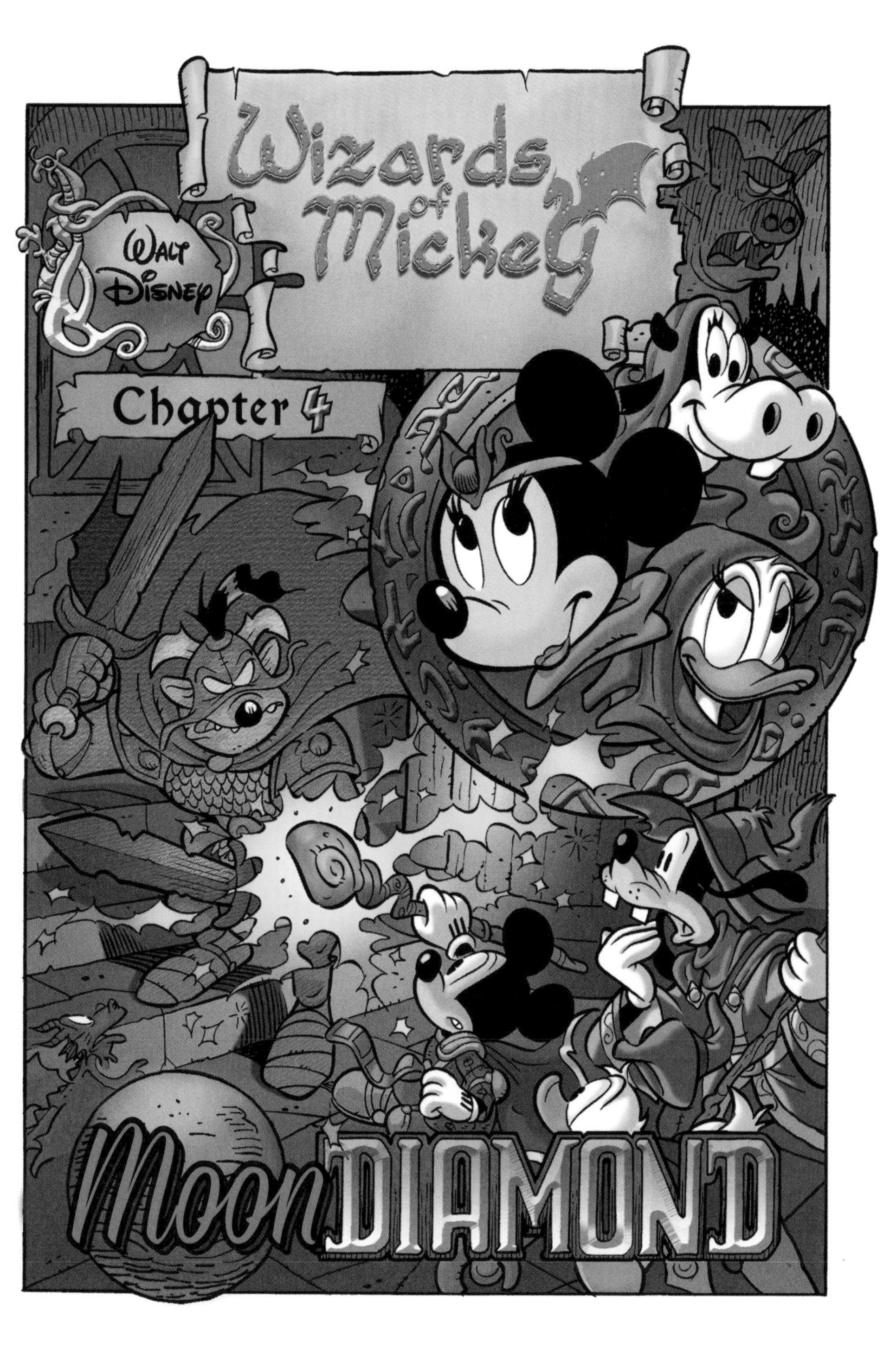
Wizards of Mickey
Walt Disney
Chapter 4
Moon DIAMOND

IT WAS THE TIME OF LEGENDS, OF WIZARDS AND HEROES... AND SPEAKING OF HEROES, HERE ARE THE ONES OF OUR ADVENTURE: THE WIZARDS OF MICKEY!
MICKEY: APPRENTICE SORCERER FROM MICELAND, HE SIGNED UP FOR THE GRAND SORCERERS TOURNAMENT TO SAVE HIS VILLAGE.
DONALD: AN UNLUCKY WIZARD. HE CAN ONLY CAST DELAYED-ACTION SPELLS.
GOOFY: HIS FAMILY WANTS HIM TO BECOME A GREAT WIZARD...BUT HE'D RATHER DO SOMETHING ELSE.
FAFNIR: A BABY DRAGON "ADOPTED" BY DONALD.
AND HERE'S THE BAD GUY!
PHANTOM BLOT, THE DUKE OF DECEPTION: HE WANTS TO CONQUER THE WORLD USING THE CROWN OF THE SUPREME SORCERER. HE COMMANDS THE BLACK PHANTOMS TEAM AND THE WEASEL GOBLINS.
THE GREAT CROWN: IT CAN ONLY BE REBUILT BY THE WIZARD WHO WINS ALL THE DIAMAGIC CRYSTALS AT STAKE IN THE GRAND SORCERERS TOURNAMENT.
THE RULES OF THE GRAND TOURNAMENT!
TEAMS OF THREE WIZARDS COMPETE IN MAGICAL CHALLENGES.
THE CHALLENGES TAKE PLACE IN THE CASTLES MARKED ON THE OFFICIAL MAP.
FOR EVERY CHALLENGE, EACH TEAM MUST STAKE THEIR DIAMAGIC.
THE WINNER TAKES THE OPPONENT'S DIAMAGIC.
THOSE LEFT WITHOUT A DIAMAGIC ARE DISQUALIFIED FROM THE TOURNAMENT.

A GREAT MAGICAL BATTLE IN CAER VANAIR CASTLE! TWO TEAMS OF SORCERERS ARE BATTLING TO WIN THE DIAMAGIC...
GAR-FOG-DIIIN! SHROUD OF MIST!

WHOA! THEY CREATED A FOG BARRIER TO HIDE FROM THEIR OPPONENTS.
WHAT A GREAT MOVE!
AND THEY'RE SO CUTE!

CUTE?! WELL, YES, BECAUSE THE THREE WIZARDS FIGHTING ARE NOT MICKEY, DONALD, AND GOOFY...
A-HYUCK! THIS MOON DIAMOND TEAM'S GREAT!
WACK! DAISY?!

AND NOW, TO FINISH THINGS OFF... ZAP-FLASH-TUUUN!

DOUBLE LIGHTNING-BOLT SPIRAL!

URGH!
ZAAAAP
OUCH!
ARGH!

WOW! AMAZING!
TSK! IT'S NO BIGGIE!
IT DOESN'T TAKE MUCH TO IMPRESS YOU NO-SCALES. THAT SPELL WOULDN'T HAVE DEFEATED A DRAGON!
I'D HAVE TURNED IT AGAINST HER, EXPLOITING THE SPELL'S WEAK POINT.
THE TWO LIGHTNING BOLTS LEAVE AN OPENING IN THE MIDDLE.
ZOT
A WELL-AIMED SPELL WOULD HIT THE SORCERESS BEFORE HER LIGHTNING COULD STRIKE!
ZAAAP
OH! I HADN'T REALIZED...
OF COURSE! YOU NO-SCALES ARE TERRIBLE WIZARDS COMPARED TO US DRAGONS.

THE ANCIENT MAGIC OF DRAGONS **MUST BE MINE**!

IF I COULD FIND THE SECRET ENTRANCE TO THEIR UNDERGROUND KINGDOM, I'D SEND MY ARMY OF WEASEL GOBLINS TO RANSACK IT...

...LIKE I DID IN ALL THE LANDS I CONQUERED!

JUST ONE OF THE DRAGONS' MAGIC SCROLLS WOULD GIVE ME MORE **POWER** THAN THE THOUSAND DUSTY BOOKS IN THE LIBRARY OF BUKARA.

THAT OLD PLACE STILL CAME IN HANDY, THOUGH...
...AS A *PRISON* FOR MY OLD ENEMY NEREUS!

HE WON'T THWART MY PLANS ANYMORE NOW THAT HE'S TRAPPED IN A MAGIC-PROOF CAGE!
ZZZ...

BUT...
PSST...MICKEY, CAN YOU HEAR ME?

Yes, Master! This *medalophone* is great for communicating long-distance!
LISTEN CLOSELY...

AS I HAVE TOLD YOU, PHANTOM BLOT HAS ***UNLEASHED*** HIS SERVANTS TO LOOK FOR THE DIAMAGIC.

So your village's Diamagic is in danger as well!
I KNOW! A SORCERER'S ALREADY TRIED TO STEAL IT!

I bet he was sent by Phantom Blot! Remember—all his servants *wear a medallion with a large "M."*

They will try anything to *trick you*. Be careful!
CRASH
THUMP
THUD

I'D BETTER
WATCH MY BACK! SOMETHING'S GOING ON...
RUMBLE
CRASH
EEEEEEK!
URGH! FAFNIR?!
C'MERE, FAFNIR!
MEOOOW!
EEEEEEK!
THUMP
THUD
CRASH
MEOOOW! HIIIISS!
SCREEK
STOP IT, KIKI! C'MERE!
MEOW!
NAUGHTY KITTY! DIDN'T I TELL YOU NOT TO CHASE AFTER LIZARDS?
PRRRR!

UMM...ACTUALLY, HE'S A BABY DRAGON!
DONALD?! WHAT A SURPRISE!

YOU'RE TELLING ME! WHEN I SAW YOU AT THE TOURNAMENT, YOU TOOK MY BREATH AWAY!
I FORMED A TEAM WITH TWO FRIENDS FROM THE SCHOOL FOR YOUNG WITCHES.

YOU GO TO A MAGIC ACADEMY?
YES! UNCLE SCROOGE SENT ME.

YOU KNOW EACH OTHER?
WELL, YEAH! WE'RE FROM THE SAME KINGDOM. WE USED TO PLAY TOGETHER AS DUCKLINGS, AND I...

Well...I always wanted to tell her... Gulp
GULP? THAT'S EASY ENOUGH TO SAY!

DAISY! COME QUICK!

CLARABELLE HAD A **PREMONITION**!
MY **CRYSTAL BALL** SHOWED ME SOMETHING VERY INTERESTING.

I GOTTA GO! MAYBE YOU CAN TELL ME WHAT YOU WERE GONNA SAY NEXT TIME.

GROAN!
HMM...

I SAW THE THREE OF US IN A TAVERN...AND A BABY DRAGON TRIED TO BEFRIEND KIKI BY BRINGING HER A NICE, FAT RAT...

BUT KIKI *REJECTED* HIM AND CHASED AFTER HIM!

BUT THAT JUST HAPPENED! WHAT KINDA *PREMONITION* IS THAT?
WELL, I SAW IT IN THE CRYSTAL BALL!

OKAY, BUT... WHEN DID YOU SEE IT?
UMM... *YESTERDAY.*

HERE WE GO AGAIN. WHAT USE ARE YOUR PREMONITIONS IF YOU *FORGET* TO TELL US?

WELL, IT'S NOT MY FAULT I'M SCATTERBRAINED.

AS LONG AS YOU REMEMBER TO *PAY* FOR THE DAMAGE YOUR CAT CAUSED!
I FORESAW THIS TOO!

THAT'S **A LOTTA MONEY**! WHERE WOULD WE EVER FIND THIS MUCH?

KITCHEN
THERE'S ALWAYS THOSE MOUNTAINS OF DISHES TO WASH.

WHAT IF I PAID YOU WITH THIS?
YOUR CROWN?!

BUT...YOU ALWAYS SAY IT'S A **PRECIOUS MEMENTO**!
I HAVE NO CHOICE!

I'M THE PRINCESS OF **MOONLAND**. I CAN'T DISGRACE MYSELF BY WASHING DISHES.

MY MASTER SAYS NO JOB IS EVER A DISGRACE WHEN IT'S USEFUL!

AND WASHING DISHES WILL KEEP YOU ON THE INNKEEPER'S GOOD SIDE.

ANYWAY, SINCE FAFNIR WAS RESPONSIBLE FOR SOME OF THE DAMAGE...
TLING
TLING

...I'LL *PITCH IN!*
TLING
TLING

THAT ALL?

I-IT'S NOT ENOUGH?

IN THE KITCHEN! GET SCRUBBING!
SWIIS

SCIAFF

HA-HA-HA!

A-HYUCK! THOSE TWO MAKE SUCH A *CUTE COUPLE*.
GOOD FOR THEM! UGH!

YOU'RE HIDING SOMETHING. AND I BET IT'S ABOUT *DAISY*!
!

SHUSH! HOW'D YOU FIGURE IT OUT?
PFFT! YOU CAN'T HIDE *LOVE TROUBLES* FROM...

...A TROUBADOUR WHO SPECIALIZES IN SERENADES!
SWISS

THAT'S YOUR NEW JOB, HUH?
YUP! YOU KNOW I NEVER WANTED TO BE A WIZARD.
PLING

MAYBE THIS IS MY TRUE CALLING!
DLENG
BLANG

I HOPE SO. I'VE TRIED TO CHARM DAISY WITH MAGICAL SERENADES BEFORE...

100

"...BUT IT ALWAYS WENT WRONG!"
MUSICUS ROMANTICUS!

OUCH! STOP! YOU GOTTA BEAT THE DRUM, NOT ME!
BONG
BONG
BONG

A-HYUCK! AS I ALWAYS SAY... NEVER RELY ON MAGIC TO SOLVE PROBLEMS!
IT'S BEST TO RELY ON FRIENDS. I'LL HELP YOU WITH DAISY!
SDLENG
SDLANG
MEANWHILE...
TO THINK I WANTED TO REST UP! TOMORROW, WE'RE UP AGAINST THE TAPESTRY TEAM.
THEY'RE POWERFUL SORCERERS! WHY'D YOU CHALLENGE THEM?
I WANNA WIN THEIR DIAMAGIC!
IT CAN CONTROL STONE.
I'M PLANNING TO USE IT TO BREAK INTO THE PRISON WHERE MY MASTER'S BEING HELD.

HMM... INTERESTING!

LATER...
THERE! THAT'S THE WINDOW OF DAISY'S ROOM. REMEMBER THE LYRICS I TAUGHT YOU... AND GET **SERENADING**!

OH, DAISY, SO FAIR... WITH FEATHERS, NOT HAIR...
DLANG
DLENG

CUT IT OUT! WHO DISTURBS THE SLEEP OF THE **TAPESTRY SORCERERS**?

HEY! IT'S ONE OF OUR **OPPONENTS**! HE WANTS TO KEEP US AWAKE BEFORE OUR CHALLENGE!
UMM... NO, NO!

THAT'S CHEATING! GET LOST, OR WE'LL HAVE YOU DISQUALIFIED!
S-SURE!
I COUNTED THE WINDOWS WRONG! AT LEAST NOW, I KNOW I'M NOT CUT OUT TO BE A MATHEMATICIAN.
THE MORNING AFTER...
TODAY'S CHALLENGE IS BETWEEN THE TAPESTRY TEAM AND THE WIZARDS OF MICKEY!
YON-WAR-POOOL! GO, WARRIOR OF TWO SWORDS!
THEY'RE ABOUT TO CAST A SPELL!

GASP! THEY BROUGHT THE WARRIOR IN THEIR TAPESTRY TO *LIFE!*
SWISSS

HE'S THEIR SECRET WEAPON! THEY LET HIM FIGHT IN THEIR PLACE, AND SINCE HE'S NOT REAL...
CLANG
CLANG
...HE NEVER GETS *TIRED.* PANT!
CLANG

SO HE'S INVINCIBLE... *WACK!*
ZAC

STRAAAAP
URK! MY POOR HAT!

IT'S RUINED!
BUT IT'S GIVEN ME AN IDEA TO BEAT THE WARRIOR.

GOOFY! **SMASH** THAT CHAIR, QUICK!

IT'LL BE EXPENSIVE. IT'S AN ***ANTIQUE***!
SWISSS

CRASH
CRASH

PERFECT! NOW... ***YEEHAW!***

THUMP

HA-HA-HA! YOU THINK TRIPPING UP OUR WARRIOR WILL STOP HIM?

NO! BUT SINCE HE'S MADE OF WOVEN THREADS...

...PULLING ONE IS ENOUGH TO UNRAVEL HIM!
VRRRR

NOOO!
AAARGH!

A-HYUCK! WHAT A NICE BALL OF YARN! ENOUGH TO MAKE SCARVES FOR ALL THREE OF US.

THE VICTORIOUS WIZARDS OF MICKEY TEAM GAINS THE STONE DIAMAGIC!

WHICH MUST BE *MINE*! THE MOON DIAMOND TEAM CHALLENGES THE WIZARDS OF MICKEY!
HUH?

VERY WELL! THE CONTEST WILL TAKE PLACE TOMORROW.

SOB! BUT I TOLD HER THIS DIAMAGIC'S IMPORTANT TO ME!
DON'T WORRY. WE'RE GONNA WIN!

THE DRAGON-SORCERERS TOLD YOU HOW TO *DEFEAT* HER SPELL, DIDN'T THEY?

THAT NIGHT...
INN
KNOCK KNOCK

>YAWN< WHO COULD THAT BE AT THIS HO—? HUH? ***CLARABELLE?!***

MINNIE HOPES THE DIAMAGIC WILL BREAK THE SPELL.
WHO CAST IT?

NO ONE KNOWS! THIS IS ALL I SAW IN MY CRYSTAL BALL.

THE MEDALLION WITH THE "M!" MINNIE'S KINGDOM WAS DESTROYED BY PHANTOM BLOT!

THAT'S TOO BAD, BUT MY FRIEND MICKEY NEEDS THAT DIAMAGIC TOO. SO...

"...DON'T EXPECT US TO GO EASY ON YOU!"
GO, MOON DIAMOND!
C'MON, WIZARDS OF MICKEY!

ZAP-FLASH-TUUUN! DOUBLE-LIGHTNING SPIRAL!

Now! Use the countermove!

UMM... YEAH! MAGICAL LIGHTN—

ZAAAP
URGH!

TSK! TOO SLOW.

I WON! THE DIAMAGIC'S MINE!
UMM...

You lether win, didn't you?

WELL, THE NEEDS OF THE MANY OUTWEIGH THE NEEDS OF THE FEW.
YOU'RE SO GENEROUS!

BUT BECAUSE YOU RAN OFF, THE KINGDOM NEEDED A NEW WIZARD, SO I WAS ALLOWED TO GO TO THE SCHOOL FOR YOUNG WITCHES.
YEAH! NOT LIKE UNCLE SCROOGE, WHO'S STILL NAGGING ME ABOUT WHAT I OWE HIM!

IT WAS MY DREAM, AND I OWE IT ALL TO YOU! YOU DESERVE A KISS!
SMACK

HEH-HEH! SOMETIMES, BEING UNLUCKY IS VERY LUCKY!
A-HYUCK! NO NEED FOR THIS THING ANYMORE.
HA-HA!
AND THAT'S HOW MICKEY MADE SOME NEW FRIENDS! BUT WILL HE MANAGE TO SAVE HIS MASTER?
THE END

Wizards of Mickey

Walt Disney
Wizards of Mickey
Chapter 5
The Well of Dragons

IT WAS THE TIME OF LEGENDS, OF WIZARDS AND HEROES...MEET THE ONES OF OUR ADVENTURE: THE WIZARDS OF MICKEY!
GOOFY: HE'S FATED TO BE A WIZARD... BUT HE'D RATHER DO SOMETHING ELSE.
DONALD: AN UNLUCKY WIZARD. HE CAN ONLY CAST DELAYED-ACTION SPELLS.
MICKEY: APPRENTICE SORCERER FROM THE VILLAGE OF MICELAND.
FAFNIR: A BABY DRAGON "ADOPTED" BY DONALD.
AND HERE'S THE VILLAIN!
THE GREAT CROWN: IT CAN ONLY BE REBUILT BY THE WIZARD WHO WINS ALL THE DIAMAGIC CRYSTALS AT STAKE IN THE GRAND SORCERERS TOURNAMENT.
THE RULES OF THE GRAND TOURNAMENT!
TEAMS OF THREE WIZARDS COMPETE IN MAGICAL CHALLENGES.
THE CHALLENGES TAKE PLACE IN THE CASTLES MARKED ON THE OFFICIAL MAP.
FOR EVERY CHALLENGE, EACH TEAM MUST STAKE THEIR DIAMAGIC.
THE WINNER TAKES THE OPPONENT'S DIAMAGIC.
THOSE LEFT WITHOUT A DIAMAGIC ARE DISQUALIFIED FROM THE TOURNAMENT.
PHANTOM BLOT: HE WANTS TO CONQUER THE WORLD USING THE CROWN OF THE SUPREME SORCERER.

THE GRAND SORCERERS TOURNAMENT HAS ARRIVED AT HANUBIS CASTLE!
ZOOT
ZAP
THE WIZARDS OF MICKEY VS THE GREEN LORDS...
KOR-GREEN-RAST! POISON IVY CLAWS!
FRUSH

URK! TO THINK I LOVE GARDENING!
NO WORRIES! I'LL FREE YOU.

RAF-CHOMP-TREEL! LOCUSTS SWARM!

BZZZZ...
CHOMP
CHOMP
CHOMP
CHOMP
CHOMP
CHOMP

NOOO!

WELL DONE! THE WIZARDS OF MICKEY WIN...

...AND GAIN THE LIGHT DIAMAGIC!
HOORAY!

WOOSH

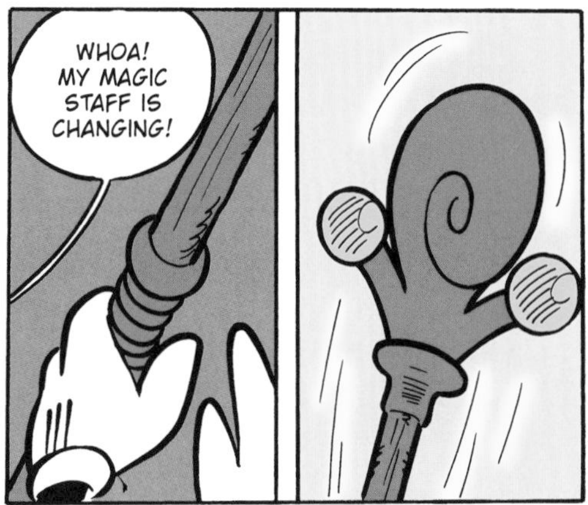
WHOA! MY MAGIC STAFF IS CHANGING!

OF COURSE! AS IT ABSORBS DIAMAGIC, ITS POWER GROWS. WHEN IT CHANGES, IT MEANS ITS OWNER...
...HAS **LEVELED UP** AS A WIZARD!
C'MERE, FAFNIR!

SO...I'M NOT A **SORCERER'S APPRENTICE** ANYMORE?
YARP!

NO! YOU'RE A **LEVEL-1 WIZARD.**
A-HYUCK! YOU GOTTA TELL YOUR MASTER!

BUT I DIDN'T TELL HIM ABOUT THE TOURNAMENT. WHAT IF HE DOESN'T APPROVE?

MY UNCLE SCROOGE IS HAPPY ABOUT IT! HE SAYS VISITING THESE CASTLES IS A GREAT OPPORTUNITY TO LOOK FOR HIDDEN TREASURES.

SO...
MASTER NEREUS, I SORT OF FORGOT TO MENTION...UMM... I SIGNED UP FOR THE GRAND SORCERERS TOURNAMENT.

Forgot?! And yet during your studies, you have never been forgetful!

HEH-HEH! DO NOT WORRY! I FIGURED IT OUT. SOME THINGS CANNOT BE HIDDEN FROM AN OLD WIZARD LIKE ME...

...EVEN IF I AM IN PRISON!

BY THE WAY, I HAVE A PLAN TO FREE YOU! I JUST NEED ONE MORE DIAMAGIC AND...

Do not risk it! Phantom Blot is too powerful for you.

TUMP
TUMP
I MUST GO! NOBODY MUST KNOW WE ARE COMMUNICATING THROUGH THE MEDALO-PHONE.

HEE-HEE! WONDER WHAT THE OLD MAN IS UP TO.
PROLLY SLEEPING, AS USUAL.
TUMP
TUMP

119

I HOPE HE HAS NIGHTMARES! HEE-HEE!
ZZZ ZZ...

ZZZ... MMRF...
HEH-HEH! THEY FELL FOR IT!

MEAN-WHILE...
NEREUS HAS NO FAITH IN ME, BUT...
VLAP
VLAP

HUH? WHAT'S GOING ON?
VLAP
VLAP
VLAP

THAT'S ***TURBO***, THE TOURNAMENT'S MESSENGER! HE'S GOT THE ***OFFICIAL MAP*** OF THE CASTLES.
VLAP
VLAP

HERE'S THE UPDATED LIST OF THE CASTLES WHERE WE CAN WIN DIAMAGIC.

WOW! THE ***LIGHTNING*** DIAMAGIC!
THE ***SWEETNESS*** ONE! YUM!
AND THE ***SEA*** DIAMAGIC!

HEY! AT THE CROW FORTRESS, WE CAN WIN THE SLEEP DIAMAGIC.
A-HYUCK! YOU HAVING TROUBLE SLEEPING?
CROW FORTRESS

I CAN HELP! I'VE STARTED WRITING LULLABIES. WANNA HEAR ONE?

I TRIED THIS ONE ON SOME FARM PIGLETS. "STOP YOUR WRIGGLING AND SLEEP LITTLE PIGLINGS..."
ZZZ

I DOUBT THAT'LL WORK ON THE WEASEL GOBLINS. IF I HAD A SLEEP DIAMAGIC, I COULD KNOCK THEM OUT...

"...LONG ENOUGH TO FREE NEREUS!"
SO THE OLD MAN TALKS IN HIS SLEEP, HUH?

YES, BOSS! HE MUMBLED, "WELL OF DRAGONS...AN ENTRANCE... VORTEX DOOR"!
WHAT MAKES YOU THINK WE CARE ABOUT A PRISONER'S RAMBLINGS?
GULP! WE'RE GONNA GET EATEN!

WE'RE LEAVING.
PETE! BEAGLE BOYS!

AT THE READY, SIR!
I'VE GOT A JOB FOR YOU!

DAYS LATER, IN THE DESERT OF SCORCHING SANDS...
PANT! CAN'T YOU CONJURE UP A BIGGER PARASOL?
WHO'S GOT SUNSCREEN?
PANT! PANT!

PANT, PANT! I DIDN'T THINK THIS MANY WIZARDS WOULD BRAVE THE DESERT TO REACH THE CROW FORTRESS.

HUFF! WHY NOT GIVE UP THE DIAMAGIC AND STICK TO LULLABIES?
THEY REALLY WORK! THE LAST ONE PUT FAFNIR TO SLEEP FOR THREE DAYS!
ZZZ...

LOOK! THE WELL OF DRAGONS OASIS!

WATER! WATER!
DO THEY SELL ICE CREAM?
RUMBLE

HALT! YOU CAN'T COME IN!
!

THE OASIS HAS BEEN CLAIMED BY THE BLACK PHANTOMS TEAM. HAR-HAR!

NO FAIR! WITHOUT WATER, WE'LL NEVER MAKE IT ACROSS THE DESERT!
YOU WANNA STOP US FROM REACHING CROW FORTRESS!

THAT'S CHEATING! WE'LL TELL THE JUDGES!

TSK! I'LL TEACH YOU A LESSON IF YOU DON'T SKEDADDLE!
HMPH! BUNCH OF BULLIES!
SO THEY DON'T SELL ICE CREAM?
HAR-HAR! SUCCESS!
Yeah! But I still don't get why Phantom Blot wants to keep the wizards...
"...AWAY FROM THE WELL!"
WE'VE BUILT THE DAM, BOSS! YOU CAN COME IN.
UNBELIEVABLE! WHO'D HAVE THOUGHT OF A SECRET PASSAGE HIDDEN IN AN OLD WELL?
HEH-HEH! WE DRAGONS ARE SMART!

AND WE CAN ALSO SENSE **DANGER**! SOMETHING FEELS WEIRD!

STOP YOUR BLITHERING, YOU **COWARD**, AND BRING NEREUS HERE.

HMPH! FINE... BUT I DON'T GET WHY YOU BROUGHT HIM ALONG.

BAH! THE DRAGONS DIDN'T KICK YOU OUT 'COS YOU'RE A **TRAITOR**...
...BUT 'COS YOU'RE SO DUMB!

NEREUS TALKED ABOUT A VORTEX DOOR. IT'S A **SEAL** ONLY A LEVEL-10 WIZARD CAN BREAK...

...CONSUMING ALL HIS POWER. I'M NOT GONNA WASTE MY ENERGY WHEN MY **OLD FRIEND** CAN DO IT FOR ME!
HMPH!

MEANWHILE...
OOF! IT'S SO HOT!
HEY, MICKEY! YOU'VE GOT THE ***RAIN DIAMAGIC***. WHY DON'T YOU USE IT?

I COULD MAKE IT RAIN IF THERE WERE CLOUDS, BUT THERE ISN'T EVEN A WISP...

TSK! ***USELESS!***
LEVEL-1 WIZARD? I'D SEND HIM BACK TO ***MAGICAL KINDERGARTEN!***

127

DON'T BE MAD! MY GREAT-GREAT GRANDPAPPY GOOFUS SOMNAMBULUS USED TO SAY, "NO SLEEP, NO DREAM"!
SNORE!
SPEAKING OF, FAFNIR'S STILL ASLEEP. DID YOU SING HIM THE ***"SLEEPING BEAUTY" LULLABY***?

AS THE HOURS PASS AND DARKNESS FALLS...

...A SECRET OPERATION BEGINS!
FRUSH FRUSH

A-HYUCK! HOW CAN WE GET WATER FROM THE WELL WITHOUT BEING SEEN?
Shhh! Be quiet!

I'VE GOT AN IDEA! I'LL TURN INVISIBLE. TRANSPARENTIS OCULI!
POF

UMM... NOTHING HAPPENED!
NO, SOMETHING DID HAPPEN...

...WE GOT BUSTED!
HEY, YOU!

SING HIM A LULLABY! MAYBE HE'LL CONK OUT, LIKE FAF-NIR!

♫ SLEEP, LI'L ♪ BEAGLE, ALL DAY 'N' NIGHT! DREAM YOU'RE IN PRISON, LOCKED UP ALL TIGHT! ♫ ♪
GRRRR!

INTRUDERS! BROTHERS, WAKE UP!

129

GRRR! GET THEM!
A-HYUCK! I'M STARTING TO THINK MY LULLABIES...
...ONLY WORK ON PETS!

GO, GO!
HUH? SNIFF! SNIFF!

YARP!
WACK! FAFNIR! WHERE'RE YOU GOING?
SWIIIS

SIGH! HE WOKE UP JUST TO TAKE A BATH?

NOT A BATH... THE WELL'S DRY!

FAFNIR COULD BE HURT. LET'S GO AFTER HIM!

GASP! THEY JUMPED IN THE WELL! WHAT DO WE DO?

WE FOLLOW THEM! IF PHANTOM BLOT FINDS OUT WE FAILED, HE'LL TURN US INTO TOADS.

MEAN-WHILE...
HERE IT IS! THE VORTEX DOOR!

REJOICE, MY WEASEL GOBLINS! SOON, THE DRAGONS' REALM WILL BE OURS!
YAAAY!
UMM... SOMETHING'S NOT RIGHT!

I WAS A GUARD IN THE KINGDOM BEFORE I JOINED PHANTOM BLOT... BUT I NEVER KNEW ABOUT THIS SECRET ENTRANCE!

AND THESE WALL PAINTINGS LOOK LIKE WARNINGS! IF ONLY I COULD SEE WHAT WAS BETWEEN THE DRAGON AND THE WELL...

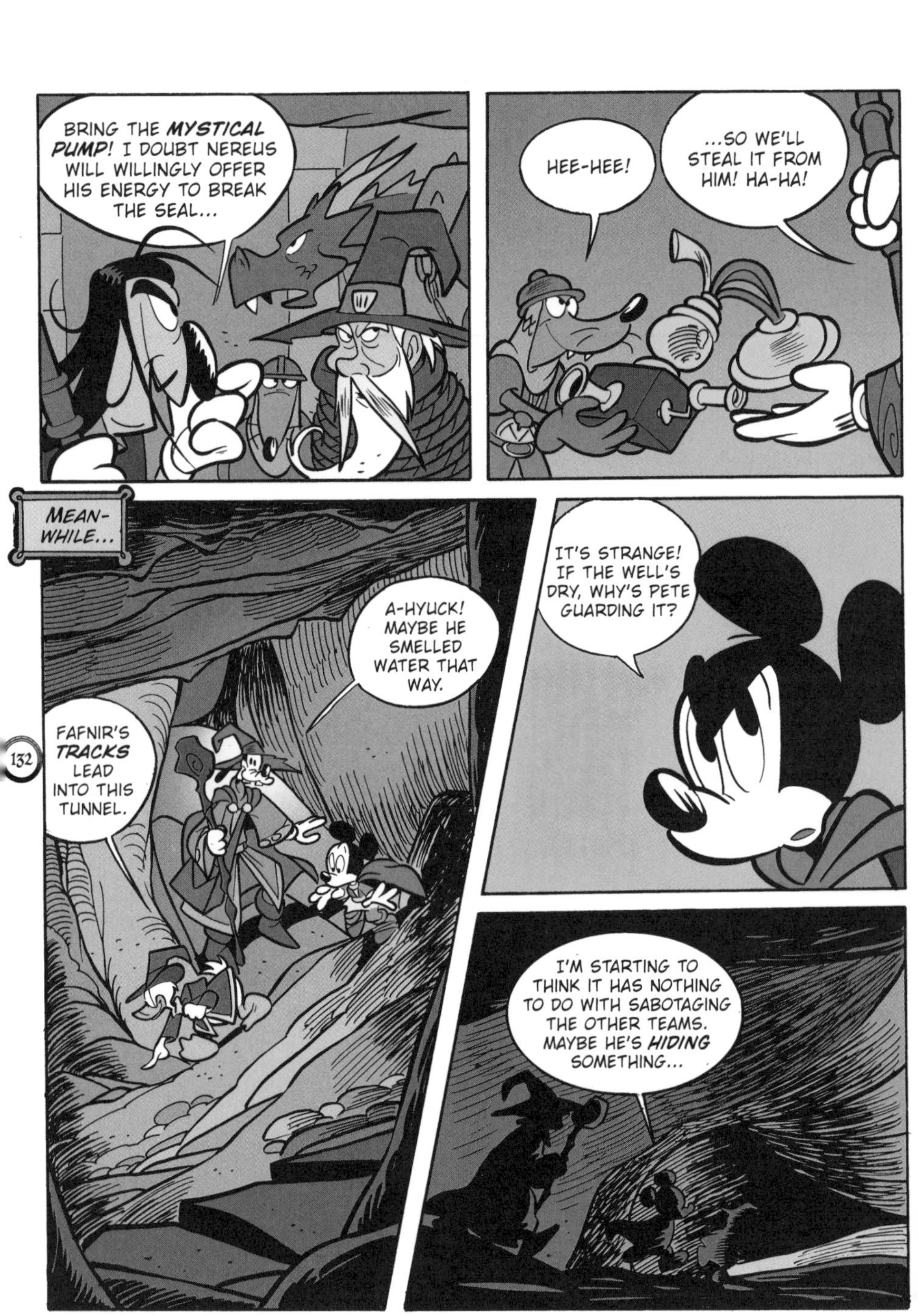
BRING THE MYSTICAL PUMP! I DOUBT NEREUS WILL WILLINGLY OFFER HIS ENERGY TO BREAK THE SEAL...
HEE-HEE!
...SO WE'LL STEAL IT FROM HIM! HA-HA!
MEAN-WHILE...
A-HYUCK! MAYBE HE SMELLED WATER THAT WAY.
FAFNIR'S TRACKS LEAD INTO THIS TUNNEL.
IT'S STRANGE! IF THE WELL'S DRY, WHY'S PETE GUARDING IT?
I'M STARTING TO THINK IT HAS NOTHING TO DO WITH SABOTAGING THE OTHER TEAMS. MAYBE HE'S HIDING SOMETHING...

"...VERY DANGEROUS!"
I'VE GOT A PLAN TO GET RID OF THE MOUSE! PUT THE INVISIBILITY CLOAK ON.

RUN PAST THOSE THREE, WITHOUT BEING SEEN...

"...AND MAKE THE BRIDGE COLLAPSE UNDER THEIR FEET!"

CRUNK

AAAH!
WACK! MY LUCK'S EVEN WORSE THAN USUAL!

A-HYUCK! WH-WHERE ARE WE?

WE'LL FIND OUT! IT'S LUCKY WE WON THE **LIGHT DIAMAGIC**.

KRiii
CACKLE
CACKLE
SNART
YEAH... REAL LUCKY. NOW I CAN SEE WHO'S ABOUT TO PLUCK AND GOBBLE ME UP! EEEP!

SING A LULLABY, GOOFY, QUICK! TIME TO FIND OUT IF THEY WORK ON ***ALL*** ANIMALS!

♪♫ YOU'RE AN UGLY, DROOLY CREEP! BUT NOW, IT'S TIME YOU FELL ♪ ASLEEP! ♫

YAAAWN!

Phew... You did it!
ZZ...
ZZ...
ZZ...
ZZ.

ZZ...
ZZ...
ZZ
Z...
ZZ
Z...
Shhh... Let's leave quietly!
Gulp! I hope Fafnir didn't bump into these monsters!
ZZ
Z...

SNIFF, SNIFF!

BONK

AHA! WHAT A SURPRISE! SO THERE ARE ACTUAL DRAGONS IN THE **WELL OF DRAGONS**.

MY EX-BROTHERS MUST'VE HIT ROCK BOTTOM IF THEY LEFT A PUPPY TO GUARD THE SECRET ENTRANCE.
HE'S THE BABY DRAGON I SAW WITH MICKEY'S FRIEND!
YARP!

IF HE'S HERE, MICKEY CAN'T BE FAR! OH NO! I DIDN'T WANT TO DRAG HIM INTO MY PLAN!

SO...
LOOK! FAFNIR! AND THERE'S ANOTHER DRAGON!

SO THAT'S WHAT HE SMELLED. HE RECOGNIZED A MEMBER OF HIS SPECIES!

AND I RECOGNIZE MY MASTER!

NEREUS?! WHAT'S HE DOING HERE?
I DUNNO! BUT IT'S THE PERFECT CHANCE TO FREE HIM.

OR TO ***JOIN HIM!*** HAR-HAR!
THUD

I'M NOT AFRAID OF YOU, PETE!
A-HYUCK! I AM, A BIT!
GRRR! INTRUDERS?!

I TOLD YOU TO STAND GUARD! NOTHING MUST THREATEN MY *TRIUMPH*!
CRiiK
CRiiK

WOOOSH
KRAAK
IT'S OPENING—IT'S... HUH? *ICE?!*

GRAAARRR!
IS THIS A JOKE, NEREUS? THIS ISN'T THE ENTRANCE TO THE DRAGONS' KINGDOM!
NO, IT IS NOT! IF YOU HAD ACTUALLY STUDIED WHEN WE WERE APPRENTICES, INSTEAD OF FOCUSING ON FORBIDDEN MAGIC...
...YOU WOULD HAVE KNOWN THAT THIS IS NOT THE WELL OF DRAGONS BUT THE WELL OF THE DRAGON *HUNTER*!
!

"A CREATURE THAT WAS IMPRISONED HERE AT THE DAWN OF TIME...
RUUUN! WE'RE NOT PAID ENOUGH TO FACE FROST GIANTS!
"...WHOSE LEGEND WAS FORGOTTEN.
"AFTER THE PAINTINGS ON THE WALLS ERODED AWAY...
"...PEOPLE FORGOT THAT THIS WASN'T AN OASIS BUT A PRISON!
I KNEW SOMETHING WAS OFF! EEEK!
CRAK
"A PRISON I LURED YOU TO BY PRETENDING TO REVEAL SECRETS IN MY SLEEP!
"YOU CALL YOURSELF THE DUKE OF DECEPTION, PHANTOM BLOT, BUT YOU FELL RIGHT INTO MY TRAP!"
NOOO!

IF I'M GONNA BE IMPRISONED, I'M TAKING YOUR FRIENDS WITH ME!
WACK!

BUT...WHERE'D HE GO?!
POF

THE INVISIBILITY SPELL JUST KICKED IN!
A-HYUCK! DELAYED-ACTION!

FOOLISH NEREUS! DID YOU THINK THE VORTEX DOOR WOULD SUCK ME INSIDE THE PRISON? MY MAGIC'S TOO STRONG!

THEN LET'S TRY A GOOD OL' SHOVE!
OOOMPH!

AAAAH!

QUICK, MICKEY! LET'S GO!
BUT...THE DOOR'S CLOSING, AND NEREUS IS STILL INSIDE!
BONK

THERE'S NO TIME TO HELP HIM. IT'S ALL COLLAPSING!

USE YOUR NOSE, FAFNIR! FOLLOW THE SCENT AND LEAD US OUTTA HERE!
SNIFF! SNIFF!

SO...
CRASH
RUMMBLE
CRACK

SOB! MY POOR MASTER!
?
BRiiiP

IT'S THE MEDALO-PHONE!
WEIRD! ONLY MY MASTER CAN USE IT...
CLAC

Walt Disney
Wizards of Mickey
Chapter 6
Witches in the Palace

IT WAS THE TIME OF LEGENDS, OF WIZARDS AND HEROES...
AND SPEAKING OF HEROES, MEET THE WIZARDS OF MICKEY!
FAFNIR: A BABY DRAGON "ADOPTED" BY DONALD.
MICKEY: A WIZARD FROM THE VILLAGE OF MICELAND.
GOOFY: FATED TO BE A WIZARD...BUT HE'D RATHER DO SOMETHING ELSE.
DONALD: AN UNLUCKY WIZARD. HE CAN ONLY CAST DELAYED-ACTION SPELLS.
TEAM MOON DIAMOND—
MINNIE: PRINCESS OF THE MOON-LAND KINGDOM. HER PEOPLE HAVE BEEN TURNED TO STONE.
DAISY: MINNIE'S CLASS-MATE AT THE SCHOOL FOR YOUNG WITCHES.
CLARABELLE: A FORTUNE-TELLER... WHO NEVER REMEMBERS HER PROPHECIES.
TOURNAMENT RULES
TEAMS OF THREE WIZARDS COMPETE IN MAGICAL CHALLENGES.
THE CHALLENGES TAKE PLACE IN THE CASTLES MARKED ON THE OFFICIAL MAP.
FOR EVERY CHALLENGE, EACH TEAM MUST STAKE THEIR DIAMAGIC.
THE WINNER TAKES THE OPPONENT'S DIAMAGIC.
THOSE LEFT WITHOUT A DIAMAGIC CRYSTAL ARE DISQUALIFIED.
THE GREAT CROWN: IT CAN ONLY BE REBUILT BY THE WIZARD WHO WINS ALL THE DIAMAGIC CRYSTALS THROUGH THE GRAND SORCERERS TOURNAMENT.

TRAVELING FROM CASTLE TO CASTLE, MICKEY AND HIS FRIENDS HAVE REACHED...
ARBOREA, THE CITY OF FLOWERS! BUY A CARNIVOROUS PLANT, ITS TRADEMARK!
MAPS TO PLAN YOUR ROUTE THROUGH THE PLANTS!
MAPS
GARDEN SHEARS!

SNIFF, SNIFF... AAA...

...CHOO!
NO FIERY SNEEZES, FAFNIR! WITH ALL THESE TREES, A FIRE WOULD DESTROY THE WHOLE CITY.

AND I CAN'T AFFORD TO RUN UP ANY MORE **DEBTS**. I ALREADY OWE UNCLE SCROOGE A FORTUNE.
BZZZZZZ

WE'RE REALLY RUNNING LOW ON CASH. I'M AFRAID WE CAN'T EVEN PAY FOR...

...THE LIFT TO THE TOP OF THE GREAT TREE, WHERE THE NEXT CHALLENGE IS BEING HELD!

WACK! YOU MEAN WE'LL HAVE TO CLIMB UP ***FIVE THOUSAND*** STEPS?

NO WORRIES.
I'VE GOT A SOLUTION!

I'VE JUST DECIDED TO START A NEW CAREER THAT'LL MAKE ME A TON OF MONEY...
VOOOSH

PAINTING!
POF

I'M GONNA START WITH SOME NICE VIEWS OF THE CITY.

AND SO...
HEY! WHAT A NICE PAINTING!

YOU CAN SEE MY HOUSE. ***I'LL BUY IT!***
TLING
TLING
TLING

AND SOON...
A-HYUCK! TEN PAINTINGS SOLD IN TEN MINUTES! IT'S A NEW RECORD!

GREAT! NOW WE CAN AFFORD A HUNDRED TRIPS ON THAT LIFT!
HEAR THAT, FAFNIR? YOU WON'T GET BLISTERS CLIMBING ALL THOSE STAIRS.
PHEEEW!

BUT...
THERE HE IS— THAT CON ARTIST!
GET HIM!
HUH?

GRRR! THE LEAVES YOU PAINTED WILTED! NOW MY HOUSE LOOKS AWFUL!

WE WANT OUR MONEY BACK!
WHAT A FRAUD!
SWISSS

SOB!
I DON'T GET IT. HOW CAN PAINTED LEAVES WILT?

HEE-HEE!
BY MAGIC! MWAH-HA-HA!
HEH-HEH!

SO IT WAS YOU! WHY'D YOU CURSE MY FRIEND'S PAINTINGS?

BECAUSE IT'S WHAT WE DO.
WE USE MAGIC TO TORMENT PEOPLE!
WHAT ELSE WOULD WITCHES DO TO PASS THE TIME?

WHY, I'LL...
KEEP YOUR FIRE-SPITTING LIZARD QUIET, OR I'LL TURN IT INTO A CENTIPEDE!

SEE YA, BUMPKIN WIZARDS! ENJOY THE STAIRS!

HMPH! I HEARD ABOUT THOSE THREE. THEY'RE TAKING PART IN THE TOURNAMENT AND CALL THEMSELVES ***TEAM JINX***!
A-HYUCK! HOW APPROPRIATE. IT'S LIKE RUNNING INTO THEM JINXED US!

WELL, LET'S GET READY TO CLIMB. THERE'S NO OTHER WAY. THE CHALLENGE IS ***TOMORROW***!

SINCE WHEN DOES THE GREAT WIZARD MICKEY GIVE UP SO FAST? WHY DON'T YOU PAY WITH ***THIS***?

A D-DIAMOND?
MINNIE? DAISY? CLARABELLE? YOU'RE HERE!
OF COURSE! COULD THE ***MOON DIAMOND*** TEAM MISS SUCH AN IMPORTANT CHALLENGE?

I THOUGHT YOU ONLY WANTED TO WIN THE ***STONE DIAMAGIC***. WEREN'T YOU GONNA USE IT TO BREAK THE SPELL THAT TURNED YOUR KINGDOM TO STONE?

UNFORTUNATELY, IT ***DIDN'T*** WORK! ***SIGH!***

"THE SPELL CAST ON MY KINGDOM IS ***TOO POWERFUL***. ONE DIAMAGIC WASN'T ENOUGH."

SO I NEED TO WIN MORE!
THE MORE WE GET, THE STRONGER OUR POWERS GROW!

SOONER OR LATER, WE'LL BE STRONG ENOUGH TO TURN THE STONES BACK INTO PLANTS AND ANIMALS.
UNCLE SCROOGE WOULD PREFER YOU TURNED THEM TO GOLD! HA-HA!

ENOUGH CHITCHAT! TO THE LIFT!
UMM...WHY'RE YOU PAYING FOR US TOO?

I HAVEN'T FORGOTTEN YOU LOST A CONTEST *ON PURPOSE* TO LET ME WIN THE STONE DIAMAGIC...

...HOPING IT COULD SAVE MY PEOPLE.

AT THE TOP...
WELCOME TO THE CASTLE OF ARBOREA! THIS CHALLENGE WILL BE *DIFFERENT* THAN THE OTHERS...

THIS WILL NOT BE A TEAM BATTLE. FOR THIS CHALLENGE, ONLY THE CAPTAIN OF EACH TEAM TAKES PART, FIGHTING ALL THE OTHER CAPTAINS!

THE *VICTOR* WILL NOT ONLY GET ALL OF THEIR OPPONENTS' DIAMAGIC, BUT ALSO THESE THREE!

NOW GO GET SOME REST... AND CHOOSE WHO AMONG YOU WILL HAVE THE *HONOR* AND *BURDEN* OF PARTICIPATING!

I'LL DO IT!
NO, I WILL! I'M THE SMARTEST!
TSK! YOU CAN'T EVEN SOLVE A **WIZDOKU***!
HEH-HEH!
*SUDOKU FOR WIZARDS

EVERYTHING'S GOING ACCORDING TO PLAN!

A-HYUCK! YOU FORMED THE TEAM, MICKEY. I SAY YOU'RE OUR CAPTAIN.

MUMBLE, MUMBLE... I HAD A PREMONITION ABOUT WHO SHOULD BE OUR CAPTAIN, BUT...

...YOU DON'T REMEMBER!
WHAT CAN I DO IF I'M SCATTERBRAINED?

BUT PICKING A CAPTAIN ISN'T EASY FOR EVERYONE...
CAAAW!
ZAP
ZIN
ZOT

SNARL! WHY SHOULD YOU BE THE BOSS, YOU ARROGANT WITCH?
GRRR! 'COS I'M MORE POWERFUL THAN YOU, YOU LOUSY SORCERESS!

I WAS TEACHING AT THE SCHOOL FOR YOUNG WITCHES WHILE YOU WERE STILL PLAYING WITH TOADS!

SO YOU ADMIT YOU'RE AN OLD SHREW?
BAH! I'M GIFTED! THAT'S WHY I STARTED TEACHING SO YOUNG!

BE QUIET!
!
ZOT
ZOT

NERAJA, WHO TOOK YOU IN WHEN YOU GOT KICKED OUT OF SCHOOL OVER YOUR FORBIDDEN EXPERIMENTS?
ERR...YOU, GARMA.

AND YOU, MAGICA? WHO STOPPED SCROOGE FROM BOMBARDING YOU WITH GARLIC?
...YOU!

AND WHO TAUGHT YOU TO USE THE MAGICAL ARTS TO TORMENT OTHERS?
YOU!

THAT'S RIGHT! SO I'M THE CAPTAIN! END OF STORY!

THAT'S WHAT YOU THINK, OLD CRONE!

MEANWHILE...
FLAP
YAAAARP!
FLAP
FLAP

MEOOW! HIIISS!
KIKI! COME BACK!

YARP?!
FAFNIR, HOW MANY TIMES DO I NEED TO TELL YOU CATS DON'T LIKE PLAYING WITH BABY DRAGONS?

SORRY, DONALD. I'M AFRAID KIKI LOVES CHASING AFTER ***LIZARDS***!

ACTUALLY, HE'S A ***DRAGON***! FROM A ***NOBLE*** LINEAGE!
HMPH!

CRAW!
FLAP FLAP
?
!

MEOOOW!
YARP!
CRAAAW!
HEH-HEH! MAYBE THEY'LL JOIN FORCES.

IN THE MEANTIME...
HMM...MINNIE'S STORY MADE ME SUSPICIOUS.

SHE DOESN'T KNOW, BUT I FOUND OUT IT WAS PHANTOM BLOT WHO TURNED HER KINGDOM TO STONE.

BUT NOW, PHANTOM BLOT'S BEEN DEFEATED. SO WHY HASN'T HIS SPELL DISSOLVED?

UNLESS...
OOF! STOP FIDGETING!

I CAN'T PAINT YOU IF YOU WON'T KEEP STILL!

WHAT DOES MICKEY SUSPECT? WE'LL FIND OUT SOON! NOW...
IS THE PLAN CLEAR, ROKNAR?

YES, MASTER! YOU'LL *LURE* THE CAPTAINS TO THE MANGROVE ARENA...
...WHERE YOU'LL *ENGAGE* THEM IN BATTLE...

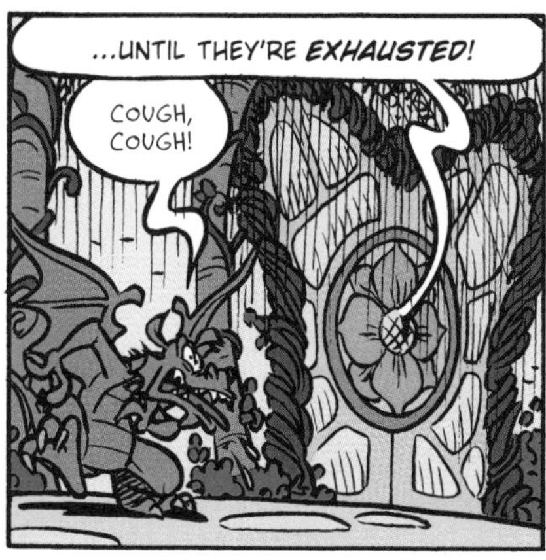
...UNTIL THEY'RE *EXHAUSTED*!
COUGH, COUGH!

THAT'S THE LAST TIME I LET YOU PLAY WITH A CAT! I BET YOU SWALLOWED A *HAIR BALL*!
COUGH! COUGH!

I SHOULD GET YOU A GLASS OF WATER...
THEN, I'LL ACTIVATE THE TELEPORTATION SPELL...

...AND STEAL THEIR *MAGIC STAFFS* WHICH CONTAIN ALL OF THEIR DIAMAGIC!
GULP!

HAVE THE WIZARDS FALLEN INTO A TRAP? LET'S SKIP TO THE NEXT DAY...
GRAUR
THE CAPTAINS WILL ENGAGE IN A MAGICAL FIGHT! THE FIRST TO MAKE IT PAST THE DRAGON GUARDING THE DIAMAGIC IS THE WINNER!

HOLD ON! DON'T YOU DARE START WITHOUT ME!

HEH-HEH! YOU'RE IN FOR A NASTY SURPRISE, YOU ARROGANT CRONE!

THE CONTEST BEGINS...
FOOOSH

NO DRAGON CAN RESIST MY MAGICAL MAGMA SOUP!

I'LL JUMP OVER THE DRAGON USING MY ENCHANTED TRAMPOLINE!

-GASP!- THIS DRAGON HAS NO TASTE!
TUNK

WHOOPS!

MWAH-HA-HA! FIRST, I'LL COVER THE OTHER WIZARDS IN BOILS, AND WHILE THEY'RE BUSY SCRATCHING...

SPUT
SPUT
N-NOTHING'S HAPPENING! WHAT'S WRONG WITH MY STAFF?

WAIT... THERE ARE NO DIAMAGIC. THESE STAFFS ARE USELESS!
SPUT
SPUT

OURS ARE WORKING, THOUGH!

AND WE'LL USE THEM TO TEACH YOU A LESSON!
ARGH! WE'RE OUTNUMBERED! WE BETTER RUN!

QUICK, TAKE OFF!

HMM...I RECOGNIZE THAT DRAGON. HE WAS WITH PHANTOM BLOT. SO, THAT VILLAIN'S STILL AROUND...

WELL DONE, MICKEY! WE STILL HAVE OUR DIAMAGIC... THANKS TO YOU!

IT'S ALL THANKS TO **DONALD**! HE DISCOVERED THE TRAP AND WARNED ME.
WELL, ACTUALLY...

"...THANK **FAFNIR**! IF HE HADN'T NEEDED A GLASS OF WATER, I'D NEVER HAVE OVERHEARD THEIR EVIL PLAN."

STILL, TRANSFERRING ALL THE DIAMAGIC INTO OUR FRIENDS' STAFFS WAS A BRILLIANT IDEA.

SO ALL HE STOLE WERE **EMPTY, USELESS STAFFS**! HEH-HEH!

YOU MEAN IF WE HADN'T **BLOCKED** THE POWER OF GARMA'S STAFF... THE WIZARD WOULD'VE STOLEN IT?
THAT'S RIGHT!

OH NO! WE MISSED OUR CHANCE TO GET RID OF THAT OLD HAG!
GRRR! IS THAT RIGHT? ***YOU'LL PAY FOR THAT!***

NOW THAT EVERYONE'S GOT THEIR DIAMAGIC BACK, WHAT DO WE DO WITH THE THREE THAT'RE UP FOR GRABS?

I SAY WE GIVE 'EM TO MICKEY. HE CAME UP WITH THE WINNING SCHEME.

AND I'LL SHARE THEM WITH MY TEAM!

SPOKEN LIKE A ***TRUE CAPTAIN***!
HEY! ***HOLD STILL***, I'M TRYING TO PAINT YOU!
THAT'S HOW MICKEY LEARNED THAT YOU DON'T HAVE TO BE THE STRONGEST TO BE A REAL CAPTAIN... YOU JUST NEED THE LOVE OF YOUR FRIENDS!
THE END

Wizards of Mickey

Wizards of Mickey
Walt Disney
Chapter 7
The Iron Dragon

IT WAS THE TIME OF LEGENDS, OF WIZARDS AND HEROES...
AND SPEAKING OF HEROES, MEET THE WIZARDS OF MICKEY!
MICKEY: WIZARD FROM THE VILLAGE OF MICELAND.
GOOFY: FATED TO BE A WIZARD...BUT HE'D RATHER DO SOMETHING ELSE.
DONALD: AN UNLUCKY WIZARD. HE CAN ONLY CAST DELAYED-ACTION SPELLS.
FAFNIR: A BABY DRAGON "ADOPTED" BY DONALD.

TEAM MAGMA FIRE!
ZAIUS, ZEFREN, AND ZORON: THREE DRAGON-SORCERERS WHO ARE COMPETING IN THE TOURNAMENT. THEY BELIEVE THAT PEOPLE (THE NO-SCALES) HAVE NO RIGHT TO USE MAGIC.

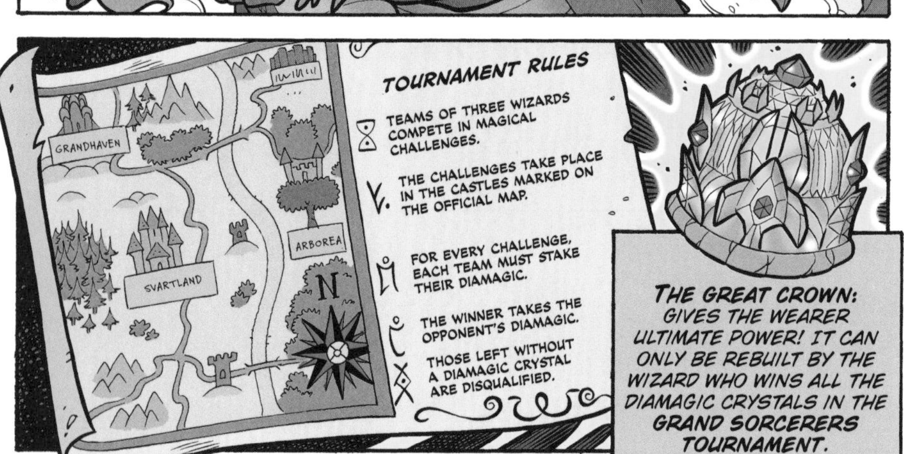
GRANDHAVEN
ARBOREA
SVARTLAND
N
TOURNAMENT RULES
TEAMS OF THREE WIZARDS COMPETE IN MAGICAL CHALLENGES.
THE CHALLENGES TAKE PLACE IN THE CASTLES MARKED ON THE OFFICIAL MAP.
FOR EVERY CHALLENGE, EACH TEAM MUST STAKE THEIR DIAMAGIC.
THE WINNER TAKES THE OPPONENT'S DIAMAGIC.
THOSE LEFT WITHOUT A DIAMAGIC CRYSTAL ARE DISQUALIFIED.
THE GREAT CROWN: GIVES THE WEARER ULTIMATE POWER! IT CAN ONLY BE REBUILT BY THE WIZARD WHO WINS ALL THE DIAMAGIC CRYSTALS IN THE GRAND SORCERERS TOURNAMENT.

AT DRUIDS CASTLE, MICKEY AND HIS FRIENDS FACE A HUGE CHALLENGE!
GO, WIZARDS OF MICKEY!
C'MON, GIANT GONZOS!
HO-HO! WE WON'T EVEN NEED MAGIC TO BEAT YOU.
WE'LL CRUSH YOU LIKE FLIES!
A-HYUCK! WE'RE GONNA NEED A LADDER!

GULP! I DON'T HAVE ONE IN MY MAGIC BAG...BUT MAYBE I CAN MAKE ONE!
WHY DON'T YOU MAKE SOMETHING TO **SHRINK** THOSE GUYS INSTEAD? DIDN'T YOU SAY YOU WANNA BE AN ***INVENTOR***?

THERE'S NO TIME! BUT I HAVE A PLAN!

LISTEN UP! PSST, PSST...

GOT IT? ***LET'S GO!***

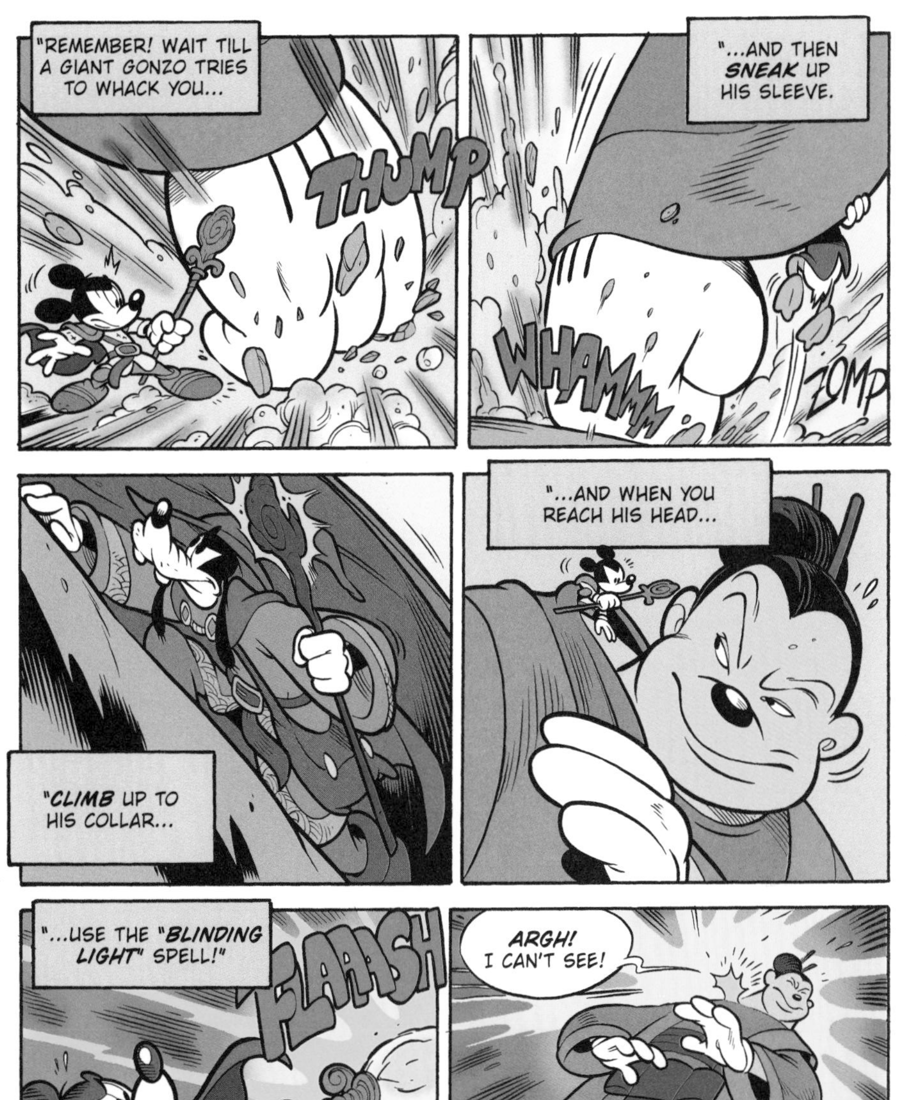
"REMEMBER! WAIT TILL A GIANT GONZO TRIES TO WHACK YOU...
THUMP
"...AND THEN **SNEAK** UP HIS SLEEVE.
WHAMMM
ZOMP
"**CLIMB** UP TO HIS COLLAR...
"...AND WHEN YOU REACH HIS HEAD...

"...USE THE "**BLINDING LIGHT**" SPELL!"
FLAAASH

ARGH! I CAN'T SEE!

17

M-ME NEITHER!
OUCH!
BONK

HERE'S THE **DIAMAGIC** YOU WON. YOU DESERVE IT!

WOW! IT'S MADE MY STAFF **EVOLVE** AGAIN!

A-HYUCK! THAT'S GREAT! NOW YOU'RE A **LEVEL-2** WIZARD!
I HEAR LEVEL-8 WIZARDS CAN TURN ROCKS TO GOLD...

IF YOU LEVEL UP QUICKLY, YOU CAN HELP ME PAY UNCLE SCROOGE WHAT I OWE HIM.
HEH HEH!

THAT NIGHT, THE WIZARDS OF MICKEY ENJOY SOME WELL-DESERVED REST...
THE PLUCKED OWL

*...BUT THEIR **DREAMS** ARE TROUBLED...*
WACK! NO...MORE DEBTS...ZZZ...
Z!

ZZZ...MY INVENTION... DOESN'T WORK... ZZZ...

ZZZ...WHO ARE YOU...? WHADDAYA WANT FROM ME? ZZZ...

SOUNDS LIKE MICKEY'S TALKING TO SOMEONE IN HIS SLEEP! LET'S SNOOP INSIDE HIS DREAM TO FIND OUT WHO...
I need your help...
WH-WHO ARE YOU?
My name is Ormen...
I'm using **telepathy** to talk to you. Come to me, and I'll explain everything...
C-COME TO YOU?
Yes! My companions will bring you here!

TUMP TUMP
BRING US... HUH?

YAWN! WHO'S KNOCKING SO LATE?
A-HYUCK! MICKEY...

...WE'VE GOT VISITORS!

I KNEW YOU'D COME! WHERE ARE YOU TAKING US?

YOU'LL KNOW WHEN YOU GET THERE. HOP IN!
SCREEEK

HEY! YOU EXPECT US TO TRAVEL IN THAT BIRDCAGE?

PLUNK
TSK! YOU WEREN'T EXPECTING TO HITCH A RIDE ON A DRAGON, WERE YOU?

HOURS LATER...
WELCOME TO MY ABODE, WIZARDS OF MICKEY.

I HOPE THE JOURNEY WASN'T TOO UNCOMFORTABLE.
WELL, IF WE HADN'T PASSED THROUGH A STORM...
STRIZZ

IN MY DREAM, YOU SAID YOU NEEDED HELP, VENERABLE ORMEN. WHAT'S UP?
YARP! YARP!
A DRAGON EGG HAS BEEN STOLEN!

NEVER BEFORE HAVE THE NO-SCALES INSULTED US DRAGONS THIS WAY. THIS COULD UNLEASH A WAR!

"LUCKILY, I CONVINCED THE **GREAT COUNCIL** TO GIVE ME SOME TIME..."
THREE DAYS! THAT'S ALL I ASK, NOBLE BROTHERS.

IF I'M UNABLE TO RETRIEVE THE EGG WITHIN THREE DAYS, GENERAL GARTH WILL HAVE FULL PERMISSION TO ATTACK THE NO-SCALES!

I SEE, BUT...HOW CAN **WE** HELP?

177

THE EGG IS IN THE FLYING CASTLE OF THE IRON SORCERERS KNOWN AS THE **ROBOT WARLOCKS**. IT'S IMPENE-TRABLE...

...AS EACH ENTRANCE IS PROTECTED BY **DEADLY TRAPS**, EXCEPT THIS **CONDUIT**. IT'S TOO NARROW FOR A DRAGON...

...BUT YOU THREE COULD CLIMB THROUGH IT INTO THE CASTLE. YOU COULD TRICK THE IRON SORCERERS LIKE YOU DID THE GIANT GONZOS!

YOU'RE GOOD FRIENDS TO US DRAGONS...THIS PUPPY IS PROOF. THAT'S WHY I'M ASKING FOR YOUR HELP.
YARP!

WE'VE GOT THIS! LET'S GET GOING!
HANG ON! YOU WANNA TRAVEL IN THE CAGE AGAIN, LIKE A CANARY?
NO WORRIES! WHILE YOU CHATTED, I BUILT...THIS! WHADDAYA THINK?
YARP!
WOW!
GASP!

I WAS INSPIRED BY THE SHAPE OF A DRAGON. IT SEEMED...AERODYNAMIC!

I'M FLATTERED!

ALL ABOARD, THEN! LET'S GO!

SO...

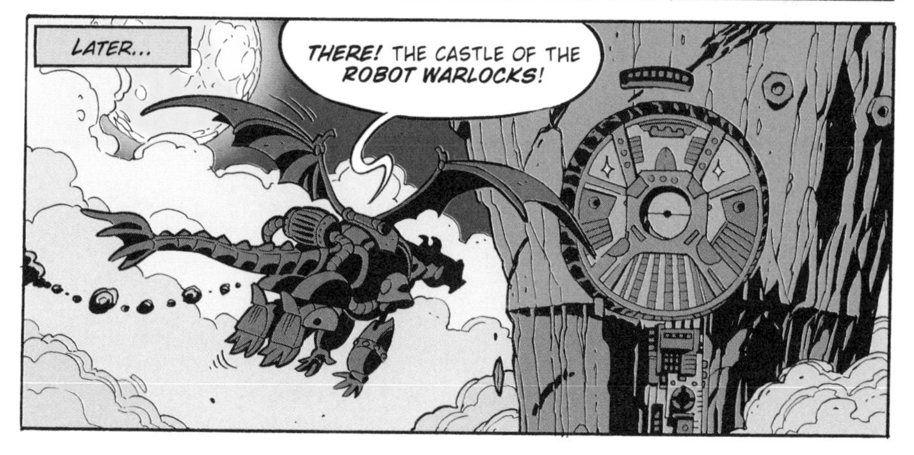
LATER...
THERE! THE CASTLE OF THE ROBOT WARLOCKS!

INSIDE...
Xius! Yron! Look! A dragon's coming!

So what, *Zulf*? It won't be able to get in...Go back to your experiments.

M
The *master* wants new weapons for his weasel goblins, and you know he's not the patient type.
He'll be pleased. This egg contains *incredible power*! Soon, we'll figure out how to extract it...

MEAN-WHILE...
OVER THERE! THAT'S THE CONDUIT!
ARE YOU READY?
SVOOOSH
PLOP

RATTLE, RATTLE...

CLANG
CLANG

HUH?
WHAT...?

A-HYUCK! DIDN'T ORMEN SAY THIS CONDUIT ***WASN'T*** UNDER SURVEILLANCE?

NOW WE KNOW DRAGONS CAN BE WRONG TOO! ***RUUUN!***

PANT, PANT...

WE'RE OUT! BUT THE ***MECHANICAL SPIDERS*** WON'T QUIT!

I'LL STOP THEM! *FER-IRON-TAL! METAL GRILLE!*

UMM... THE CONDUIT'S STILL OPEN... AND THE SPIDERS ARE STILL COMING!
SOB! WHY DO MY SPELLS ***NEVER*** WORK WHEN THEY SHOULD?

WE'VE NO TIME TO LOSE! ***LET'S MOVE!***
!

SOON AFTER...
DID WE LOSE THEM?
LOOKS LIKE IT...

...EEEK!

RELAX! IT'S NOT A REAL WOLF... IT'S MADE OF METAL.
TONG TONG

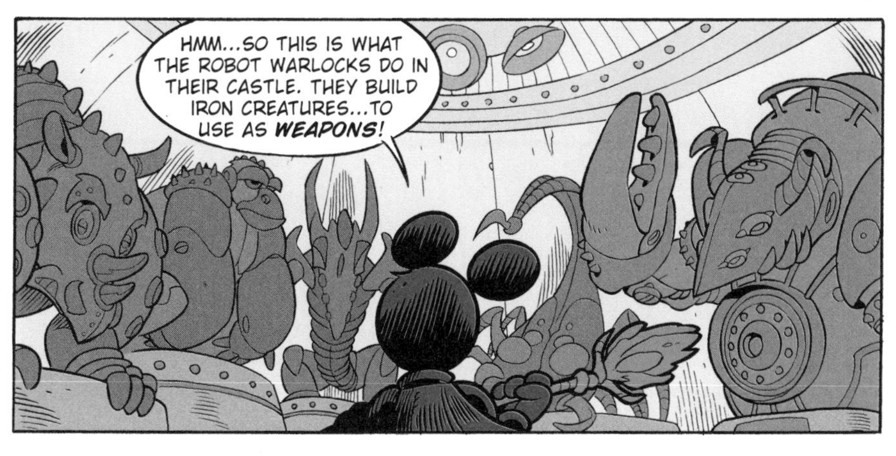
HMM...SO THIS IS WHAT THE ROBOT WARLOCKS DO IN THEIR CASTLE. THEY BUILD IRON CREATURES...TO USE AS WEAPONS!

A-HYUCK! AND HERE ARE THE ANIMALS THEY'VE USED AS EXPERIMENTS.
SNIFF SNIFF
INCREDIBLE!
HORRIBLE, I'D SAY.

WE GOTTA **FREE** THEM! LET'S SPLIT UP. YOU GUYS HANDLE THE CAGES— I'LL LOOK FOR THE EGG!

I THINK FAFNIR'S ALREADY ON THE SCENT.

Connect it to the *positive* terminal, Xius.
You mean *negative*!

Don't be silly! You wanna blow everything up like that doofus Zulf did?

How dare you? *My* experiments never fail. I'm way smarter than you both!

Oh yeah? Then why'd you always copy my homework in magic school?
Grrr!

I'VE GOT AN IDEA. LET'S BREAK THE ***LOCKS*** OF THE CAGES!
ZAAAP
CRACK
CRACK

MUUUU
CROOOAK
IIIIIIH
ROAAARRR
Hey! What's going on in there?

Argh! The animals are escaping... *Oomph!*

Oh no! I bet it's your fault, Yron! You forgot to *lock* the doors!

I couldn't have forgotten them all! Someone's *opened* them!

THAT'S RIGHT! I NEEDED TO GET TO THE EGG UNDISTURBED! AND NOW...

CATCH, GOOFY!
SWISSS

Fools! You won't make it out of the castle! *METALLIC...*

...FUSION...

...SPELL!

Let's catch them!
No, let's crush them!
PFFFT
No! Let's disintegrate them!
PFFFT
PFFFT
GASP! THEY'VE TRANSFORMED INTO A GIANT ROBOT WARLOCK!
HMM...THOSE THREE DEFINITELY ***DON'T*** GET ALONG. I'VE GOT AN IDEA...

RUN IN OPPOSITE DIRECTIONS AND... ACCUSE ONE ANOTHER!

PANT! LET'S HOPE THEY CHASE GOOFY! HE'S GOT THE EGG!

PUFF! GO AFTER DONALD! HE'S THE STRONGEST!

PANT! NOT ME! MICKEY! HE'S THE BOSS!

Hear that? Let's hit the one on the right!
No! The one on the left!
It's the one in the middle, idiots!

Who's an idiot?
I'm the boss!
No way!

HEH-HEH! IT WORKED! IF THEY ARGUE, THE FUSION SPELL BREAKS!
TUMP
ZAC

AND NOW...BACK TO OUR DRAGON!
SWISSS

OH NO! THE GRILLE! CURSE MY DELAYED-ACTION SPELLS!

THEN IT'S TIME TO TRY MY NEW REMOTE-CONTROLLED INVENTION ON THE DRAGON.

BZZZ
?

BZZZ

FOOOSH

FOOOSH
IT WORKED!

QUICK! LET'S TAKE THE ANIMALS WITH US!

FLY, BUDDY!
NEIGH!

AND SO, AFTER LOADING UP THE ANIMALS THEY'D RELEASED FROM THE ROBOT WARLOCKS' CASTLE ON THEIR IRON DRAGON...
THANK YOU, MICKEY! THREE NO-SCALES RISKING THEIR LIVES TO SAVE A DRAGON EGG WILL CONVINCE MANY DRAGONS THAT OUR SPECIES CAN BE FRIENDS.

WHAT'S ON YOUR MIND, GOOFY? IS SOMETHING WORRYING YOU?
I WAS THINKING ABOUT THE ROBOT WARLOCKS. THEIR INVENTIONS WERE FOR EVIL PURPOSES...

...SO BEING AN INVENTOR IS BAD!
BUT THE REMOTE-CONTROLLED DEVICE YOU INVENTED SAVED OUR LIVES!

191

RIGHT! REMEMBER—TECHNOLOGY ITSELF ISN'T GOOD OR BAD. IT DEPENDS ON HOW YOU USE IT!
HEH HEH!
PANT! I SUGGEST A GREAT INVENTION—A FOOD DISPENSER FOR ANIMALS! PUFF!
THE TOURNAMENT CONTINUES!

THE END

Wizards of Mickey

Wizards of Mickey
Walt Disney
Chapter 8
The Monster Hunters

IT WAS THE TIME OF LEGENDS, OF WIZARDS AND HEROES...
AND SPEAKING OF HEROES, MEET THE WIZARDS OF MICKEY!
MICKEY: WIZARD FROM THE VILLAGE OF MICELAND!
GOOFY: FATED TO BE A WIZARD...BUT HE'D RATHER DO SOMETHING ELSE.
DONALD: AN UNLUCKY WIZARD. HE CAN ONLY CAST DELAYED-ACTION SPELLS.
FAFNIR: A BABY DRAGON "ADOPTED" BY DONALD.
AND HERE ARE THE VILLAINS: THE BLACK PHANTOMS! ONE OF THE BEAGLE BOYS HAS AN INVISIBILITY CLOAK.
TOURNAMENT RULES
TEAMS OF THREE WIZARDS COMPETE IN MAGICAL CHALLENGES.
THE CHALLENGES TAKE PLACE IN THE CASTLES MARKED ON THE OFFICIAL MAP.
FOR EVERY CHALLENGE, EACH TEAM MUST STAKE THEIR DIAMAGIC.
THE WINNER TAKES THE OPPONENT'S DIAMAGIC.
THOSE LEFT WITHOUT A DIAMAGIC CRYSTAL ARE DISQUALIFIED.
THE GREAT CROWN: THE TOOL OF ULTIMATE POWER! IT CAN ONLY BE REBUILT BY THE WIZARD WHO WINS ALL THE DIAMAGIC CRYSTALS IN THE GRAND SORCERERS TOURNAMENT.

IT'S A LIVELY NIGHT IN SILVERLEAF FOREST...
THERE! THE GHOST WARRIOR!
AAAH! I DON'T WANNA SEE HIM! HIS UGLY FACE WILL GIVE ME NIGHTMARES!
ACTUALLY, HE'S INVISIBLE... OR WHAT KINDA GHOST WOULD HE BE?!

SWISSS
QUICK! ATTACK!

UR-ZAT-CAAAGE! MYSTICAL CAGE!

AAARGH!
GO BACK TO THE SHADOW WORLD!

CLANG
THUD

Y-YOU DID IT!
THE G-GHOST IS...GONE?
YOU'RE HEROES!
YEAH! AND YOU THINK THE HEROES ARE MICKEY AND HIS FRIENDS, RIGHT?

WRONG!
HAR-HAR! NO HORRID CREATURE CAN ESCAPE THE BEST MONSTER HUNTERS IN THE COUNTY.

C'MON, RETRIEVE THE WARRIOR'S ARMOR!

YOU DON'T MIND IF WE TAKE IT, RIGHT? WE ALWAYS KEEP SOUVENIRS OF OUR MISSIONS.
YOU SAVED MY VILLAGE ...

I DUNNO HOW TO THANK YOU!
GIMME THE THOUSAND DOUBLOONS YOU PROMISED!
SWISSS

THEY'RE ALL THERE. YOU CAN CHECK.
TSK! I TRUST YOU. I ONLY DO BUSINESS WITH GENTLEMEN, LIKE MY-SELF!
TLING

WELL, GOOD-BYE! AND IF A NEW MONSTER SHOWS UP...

...HERE ARE OUR BUSINESS CARDS!
YOU THINK THEY CAN MAKE MY WIFE'S MEAT LOAF DISAPPEAR? IT'S REALLY **MONSTROUS**!

LATER...
MWAH-HA-HA! WE'VE NEVER MADE SO MUCH EASY MONEY!
TLING
TLING

YOU'RE A GENIUS, PETE!
HAR-HAR! THAT'S RIGHT...
TLING

HEY! WHAT ABOUT MY SUPERB ACTING?
FRUSH
FRUSH

I PRACTICED MY GHOSTLY SCREAMS FOR THREE DAYS.

QUICK! PUT THE INVISIBILITY CLOAK IN THE BAG WITH THE ARMOR!

NEXT TIME, I WANNA BE THE GHOST WARRIOR. TERRORIZING VILLAGERS IS A HOOT! HA-HA!

FOR ME, THE FUN IS GETTING PAID TO DEFEAT A MONSTER THAT DOESN'T EXIST! HAR HAR!
IT DOESN'T EXIST? ARE YOU SURE, PETE?
ELSE-WHERE...
FRUSH
FRUSH
FRUSH
RRRRRRR
YIP!
DAYS LATER, AT SUNSET...
THIS WHEAT FIELD'S HUGE. I HOPE MY PEGASUS DOESN'T CATCH HAY FEVER.
NEIGH!

SIGH! WALKING IN THIS FIELD REMINDS ME OF MY CHILDHOOD IN MICELAND...
"MY FAVORITE GAME WAS DIGGING UP MOLES WITH PLUTO...
SNIFF, SNIFF!
"I'D PRETEND TO TURN THEM INTO GOBLINS..."
WOOF, WOOF!
YIP!
HEH-HEH! GUESS I WAS DESTINED TO BECOME A SORCERER.
SOB! AS A DUCKLING, I DREAMED OF DOING MAGIC TOO...
I WANTED TO MULTIPLY MY **POCKET MONEY** TO BUY TOY SOLDIERS. UNCLE SCROOGE WAS SUCH A PENNY-PINCHER...
HERE WE ARE! THE FORTRESS CITY OF **BLACK-BURG**!

HERE THEY ARE! HOORAY!
GREETINGS, *MILORDS!*
PEREPEEE
?

A-HYUCK! WHAT A WELCOME!

WE'VE BEEN AWAITING YOUR ARRIVAL. THE CITY DESPERATELY NEEDS YOUR HELP!
HUH?

OUR HELP? WHAT FOR?
AREN'T YOU THE **MONSTER HUNTERS**?

THOSE THREE LOSERS? DON'T BE SILLY!

YOU ASKED FOR THE BEST, AND WE'VE COME...*IN A FLASH*! HAR-HAR!
GULP!

THE BLACK PHANTOMS? YOU'RE STILL IN THE TOURNAMENT EVEN AFTER YOUR BOSS, PHANTOM BLOT, WAS DEFEATED?

WHO SAID ANYTHING ABOUT THE TOURNAMENT? WE'RE HERE ON **BUSINESS**!

A MONSTER'S BEEN HANGING AROUND HAWK PASS LATELY, AND THE TOWN CHIEF IS AFRAID IT'LL COME HERE.
IT WAS HEARD HOWLING IN THE FIELDS NEAR ROGUE FALLS, THE OWL CITADEL, AND THE RED CASTLE...

IF IT KEEPS FOLLOWING THAT ROUTE, BLACKBURG'S NEXT! GULP!
ROGUE FALLS
OWL CITADEL
RED CASTLE
BLACKBURG
LAKE
ELF

SO YOU CALLED ME AND MY ASSOCIATES TO PROTECT THE CITY!
OOOMPH!
PAF

AT A COST, OF COURSE. HALF NOW, HALF AFTER THE JOB'S DONE.
TLING

SEE YA, MOUSE! US PROFESSIONALS HAVE WORK TO DO.

HMM... SOMETHING SMELLS FISHY.
WELL, LET'S GO GET READY, MICKEY.

WE'RE HERE FOR ANOTHER MATCH AGAINST THE TAPESTRY WIZARDS! WE'D BETTER EAT BEFORE THE CHALLENGE!

MEAN-WHILE...
UMM...SORRY, PETE. YOU REALLY WANNA WAIT FOR THE MONSTER TO SHOW UP?

HMPH! EXPLAIN THE PLAN TO YOUR IDIOT BROTHER.

NOBODY KNOWS WHAT THE MONSTER LOOKS LIKE, SO ONE OF US WILL PRETEND TO BE IT.
THUD
OUCH!

THEN WE'LL ACT LIKE WE CAUGHT IT AND LEAVE WITH THE CASH BEFORE THE REAL MONSTER SHOWS UP!
SOCK
OW!

SHORTLY AFTER...
HEY! WE DON'T SERVE **LIZARDS**!

ACTUALLY, HE'S A DRAGON.
TSK! AND I'M A **FAIRY**! I SAID, GET OUT!

I'LL TAKE HIM TO THE STABLES WITH PEGASUS. YOU START ORDERING— I'M STARVING!

LET'S CHECK OUT THE MENU—WAIT! WHY'RE YOU DOODLING ON IT?

THEY'RE NOT DOODLES. IT'S A **MAP** OF THE LANDS WE'VE CROSSED!
Menu

I THINK I'VE FOUND MY NEW CALLING. I'LL BE A **CARTOGRAPHER**!
Menu

DRAWING MAPS IS SUCH A USEFUL JOB. YOU DISCOVER LOTS OF COOL STUFF!
FOR INSTANCE, THE MONSTER HAS BEEN FOLLOWING THE EXACT SAME ROUTE AS US, PASSING EVERY CASTLE WHERE CONTESTS HAVE BEEN TAKING PLACE.
HMM...WEIRD. IT'S ALMOST LIKE IT'S...
Menu
"...FOLLOWING US!"
RRRRRRRS
AT THAT MOMENT...
HORSERADISH AND GARLIC SOUP! OUR SPECIALTY!
SNIFF, SNIFF... BLEAH!

Hey, stop stuffing your faces. Let's fight!
!

THE TAPESTRY WIZARDS?!
HEH-HEH! I LOVE THE TALKING-BOWL TRICK!

C'MON! GET YOUR DIAMAGIC READY. IT'S TIME FOR OUR MATCH!

BUT WE JUST GOT HERE AND WE NEED TO REST. CAN'T WE DO IT TOMOR-ROW?

NO CAN DO! CONTESTS ONLY TAKE PLACE IN BLACKBURG AT NIGHT WHEN THE MOON IS FULL!

THAT'S THE RULE. IF YOU DIDN'T KNOW THAT, TOO BAD!

WE'LL BE WAITING IN THE ARENA. DON'T BE LATE!
HMPH! THEY JUST WANNA CHALLENGE US WHILE WE'RE TIRED.
I FINALLY SETTLED FAFNIR DOWN. IT'S CHOW TIME...HUH?
HEY! WHERE ARE YOU GOING? I HAVEN'T EATEN YET!
NEITHER HAVE WE. BUT IT'S TIME FOR THE MATCH!
AND SO...TAPESTRY WIZARDS VS THE WIZARDS OF MICKEY!
GROAN! MY SPELLS ARE EVEN WORSE THAN USUAL ON AN EMPTY STOMACH!

ZAR-WAR-POOL! EIGHT-ARMED WARRIOR!
IT'S THEIR USUAL TACTIC! THEY'RE SENDING THE WARRIOR **WOVEN** ON THE TAPESTRY TO FIGHT IN THEIR PLACE!

AND WE'LL DEFEAT IT LIKE LAST TIME... BY **UNRAVELING** IT!
SWOSSSH
ZING

HUH?
MY ENCHANTED KNITTING NEEDLES DIDN'T WORK!
SNIK

I'LL TRY BURNING THE FABRIC! GER-LON-FIIIRE! SCORCHING FLAME!

WOOOSH

A-HYUCK! THAT DIDN'T WORK EITHER!

HA-HA-HA! OUR WARRIOR'S FABRIC IS FIREPROOF AND RESISTANT TO RIPS.

YOU'RE DOOMED!

FRUSH
FRUSH

AAAH!
HEEELP! IT'S THE MONSTER!
RARRR
URGH!
ZAMP
IT'S HERE!
!

HOLD IT BACK WITH FIRE!

IT'S ESCAPING! CALL THE **MONSTER HUNTERS**!
YIP!

YOU GOT LUCKY, BUMPKIN WIZARDS! BUT NEXT TIME, WE'LL WIPE THE FLOOR WITH YOU!

GRRR!
EASY, FAFNIR! I KNOW YOU WANNA PROTECT ME, BUT RIGHT NOW, WE GOTTA RUN!

HUH? WHAT DID YOU SAY? ***PROTECT YOU?!***

OF COURSE! HOW DID I NOT SEE IT? ***I KNOW WHO THE MONSTER IS!***

FOLLOW ME! WE GOTTA FIND HIM BEFORE THE HUNTERS HURT HIM!
WHAT IF HE HURTS US? GULP!

HE WON'T. WHEN HE JUMPED OUT OF THE BUSHES, HE DIDN'T WANT TO ATTACK ME...

...HE WANTED TO **PROTECT ME**. JUST LIKE FAFNIR DOES WITH DONALD.

THAT'S NOT A MONSTER...

...THAT'S MY OLD FRIEND **PLUTO**!
YIP!

HE ACCIDENTALLY DRANK A **WEREWOLF POTION** WHEN HE WAS A PUPPY, BUT IT DIDN'T SEEM TO HAVE ANY EFFECT.
SLAP
SLAP

IT WAS PROBABLY DELAYED-ACTION, JUST LIKE MY SPELLS.

A-HYUCK! AND WHEN HE SAW YOU IN DANGER, HE **TRANS-FORMED** TO HELP YOU!

YEAH! I SUSPECT HE'S DONE IT SEVERAL TIMES SINCE LEAVING MICELAND TO LOOK FOR ME.
TO LOOK FOR YOU?

YEAH! I THOUGHT IT WAS ODD THAT THE "MONSTER" HAD FOLLOWED OUR TRAIL DURING THE TOURNAMENT...

...AND WHEN I FIGURED OUT IT WAS PLUTO, I SOLVED THE MYSTERY. HE WAS ACTUALLY FOLLOWING ME!
POOR PLUTO! I BET HE FELT LONELY IN MICELAND.

MEAN-WHILE...
IS THE PLAN CLEAR?
YES, PETE!

HMPH! THE MONSTER SHOWED UP EARLY...BUT WE'LL USE THAT TO OUR ADVANTAGE!

PANT! WE DID IT! WE CAUGHT THE MONSTER!

HOW CAN I BE SURE IT'S INSID—? OH DEAR!
GRRR! ROOOWR! RAAAR!

WELL, IF YOU WANNA OPEN IT UP TO CHECK...
NO, THAT'S OKAY! HERE'S YOUR MONEY!
ROAAAR

HOLD ON, SIR! PETE'S NOT A PROFESSIONAL MONSTER HUNTER BUT A PROFESSIONAL SWINDLER!

HOW DARE YOU, MOUSE? YOU WANNA OPEN THE CAGE?
YEAH! GIVE IT A TRY!

I DON'T NEED TO 'COS THE **REAL MONSTER** IS HERE WITH ME!
WOOF!

PLUTO, **TRANSFORM**!
ROOOWL!

URGH!
AAAH!

RUUUN!!
HEY! DON'T LEAVE ME IN HERE!
HEY! COWARDS! LIARS! **GET THEM!**

SOB!
GRRR!

YOU'RE SO BRAVE! NOT ONLY DID YOU STOP THE MONSTER, YOU *TAMED* IT. YOU DESERVE A REWARD!

KEEP YOUR MONEY! IT WASN'T HARD...HE'S JUST A BIG *PUPPY*!
BLINK

THAT'S TRUE!
HE'S SO CUTE!
HEH-HEH! YEAH! NEVER TRUST APPEARANCES...

"EVEN THE TAPESTRY WARRIOR SEEMS INVINCIBLE...
LET'S PICK UP WHERE WE LEFT OFF, MOUSE!
"...BUT IT'S JUST A PIECE OF WOVEN FABRIC.
KREL-GUM-BLOCK! IMPENETRABLE BUBBLE!
"SO IF WE SURROUND THE TAPESTRY WITH A MAGIC BUBBLE, IT'LL BE TRAPPED!"
NOOO!
WE LOST AGAIN!
AND I WON THE GREATEST PRIZE—AN OLD FRIEND!
WOOF!
THE END

Wizards of Mickey
Chapter 9
THE RETURN OF PHANTOM BLOT
WALT DISNEY

IT WAS THE TIME OF LEGENDS, OF WIZARDS AND HEROES...
MEET THE WIZARDS OF MICKEY!
DONALD: AN UNLUCKY WIZARD. HE CAN ONLY CAST DELAYED-ACTION SPELLS.
FAFNIR: A BABY DRAGON "ADOPTED" BY DONALD.
MICKEY: WIZARD FROM THE VILLAGE OF MICELAND.
GOOFY: FATED TO BE A WIZARD...BUT HE'D RATHER DO SOMETHING ELSE.
PHANTOM BLOT: HE WANTS TO BECOME THE SUPREME SORCERER...AT ALL COSTS. HE COMMANDS THE WEASEL GOBLINS AND THE TERRIBLE DRAGON ROKNAR.
THE GREAT CROWN: GIVES THE WEARER ULTIMATE POWER! IT CAN ONLY BE REBUILT BY THE WIZARD WHO WINS ALL THE DIAMAGIC CRYSTALS IN THE GRAND SORCERERS TOURNAMENT.
TOURNAMENT RULES
*TEAMS OF THREE WIZARDS COMPETE IN MAGICAL CHALLENGES.
*THE CHALLENGES TAKE PLACE IN THE CASTLES MARKED ON THE OFFICIAL MAP.
*FOR EVERY CHALLENGE, EACH TEAM MUST STAKE THEIR DIAMAGIC.
*THE WINNER TAKES THE OPPONENT'S DIAMAGIC.
*THOSE LEFT WITHOUT A DIAMAGIC CRYSTAL ARE DISQUALIFIED.

THE WIZARDING TEAMS PARTICIPATING IN THE GRAND SORCERERS TOURNAMENT HAVE GATHERED AT THE CASTLE OF A THOUSAND ROOMS...
THEY'RE NOT HERE FOR A CHALLENGE BUT...
SOUP'S READY!

...FOR A PARTY!
YUM!
READY TO TRY THE SPECIAL RECIPE OF TEAM YUM-YUM COOK?
TOTALLY!
CUCIN

HMPH! YOU'VE ALREADY EMPTIED HALF THE CAULDRON, JUST CHECKING IF IT WAS READY!

A-HYUCK! A PARTY TO MEET THE OTHER CONTESTANTS IS JUST THE TICKET. DAISY HAD A GREAT IDEA!

WELL, GRANDMA DUCK ALWAYS SAID IT TAKES A REAL LADY TO ORGANIZE A GREAT PARTY!
AND SHE TAUGHT ME ALL HER SECRETS!

THEN WHY DIDN'T YOU STICK TO PLAYING GRANDE DAME IN YOUR CASTLE INSTEAD OF PRETENDING TO BE A WITCH?
HMPH! THINK YOU'RE BETTER THAN ME, NERAJA?

OBVIOUSLY...SINCE I WAS YOUR *TEACHER* AT THE SCHOOL FOR YOUNG WITCHES!

BUT YOU GOT KICKED OUT! WONDER WHY...
GRRR! THAT'S NONE OF YOUR BUSINESS, YOU *QUACKER*!

DON'T LISTEN TO HER, DAISY. SHE'S JUST JEALOUS!
CALM DOWN...

WE'RE HERE TO HAVE FUN, NOT FIGHT—.
EEEEK!

THERE'S A *LIZARD* IN THE CAULDRON!
BLEAH!

BLUB
BLOB
BLUB
OH NO! WHAT'RE YOU DOING, FAFNIR? THAT'S OUR SOUP, NOT YOUR HEATED SWIMMING POOL!

URGH!
HAR-HAR! MY COMPLIMENTS TO THE CHEF!
SUCH A FANCY PARTY! MWAH-HA-HA!

PETE?! WHY'RE YOU HERE? HOW'D YOU GET OUTTA BLACKBURG PRISON?
WHO WANTS THE FIRST TASTE?
EEEK!

WELL, I MAGICALLY CONVINCED THE JUDGE I WAS INNOCENT! HEH-HEH!
IF NOBODY WANTS IT, I'M GONNA DIG IN...SLURP!
BURP SLURP GURGLE CIOMP
GNAM

TSK! DID YOU BREAK OUT?
HMM...THE PROBABILITY OF BUSTING OUT OF A JAIL WITH LOADS OF GUARDS IS LESS THAN 0.01%!

HUH?
A-HYUCK! I DECIDED TO TAKE UP **STATISTICS**!

MAYBE THAT'S MY VOCATION. I DON'T WANNA BE A WIZARD...

"...BUT I GOTTA FIND A **JOB**, OR WHAT AM I GONNA TELL MY FAMILY WHEN I GO HOME?"

BAH! GO **CALCULATE THE PROBABILITY** OF FINDING A JOB ELSEWHERE!
THUMP
!

I WANT A SLICE OF CAKE!
CLANG

SO YOU DIDN'T BREAK OUT, HUH? YOU'VE STILL GOT THE...TOOLS OF THE TRADE!

HMPH! GIVE IT BACK, YOU BUSYBODY!
ZAF

THIS BUMPKIN WIZARD'S CALLED ME A LIAR! I'M NOT GONNA SPEND ANOTHER SECOND IN HIS PRESENCE!
WELL SAID, PETE! LET'S GO BE OUTRAGED IN OUR ROOMS!

DON'T MIND THOSE BULLIES, MICKEY. ENJOY THE PARTY!
HMM...

"SOMETHING'S NOT ADDING UP."
HAR-HAR! IT'S ALL GOING ACCORDING TO PLAN!

PLAN?! WHAT IS THE **BLACK PHANTOMS TEAM** PLOTTING? YOU'LL FIND OUT SOON! WE'LL HAVE TO GO BACK A FEW DAYS...
GROAN! I'VE SEEN PLENTY OF PRISONS IN MY CRIMINAL CAREER, BUT BLACKBURG IS THE WORST!

...HARD BEDS, YUCKY FOOD...

...AND THE LIGHT WENT OUT WHILE I WAS DRAWING!

THE LIGHT?! HEY, HOW CAN THE MOON **SWITCH OFF**?
IT D-DIDN'T...

...IT DIDN'T SWITCH OFF! **L-LOOK!**

ROKNAR?!
PHANTOM BLOT'S DRAGON? WHAT'S HE DOING HERE?

I'M BUSTING YOU FOOLS OUT OF JAIL. THE MASTER NEEDS YOU!
FOOOSH

FOOOOOSSSSHHH
DUCK!

SO...
PETE! BEAGLE BOYS! EVEN THOUGH YOU'VE LET ME DOWN IN THE PAST, I STILL NEED YOU.

IN DISGUISE, I'VE BEEN MINGLING WITH THE WIZARDS TAKING PART IN THE TOURNAMENT...

...AND I DISCOVERED THEY PLAN TO GATHER AT THE CASTLE OF A THOUSAND ROOMS! JOIN THEM AND...

Psst, psst, psst...
HEH-HEH! **WICKED!**

NOW, **GO!** AND DON'T LET ME DOWN AGAIN!

UMM...DID ANYONE ASK HOW HE CAME BACK AFTER BEING BANISHED TO **ANOTHER DIMENSION**?

THERE ARE SOME THINGS I'D RATHER NOT KNOW, BROTHER!

YOU'LL SOON FIND OUT. BUT LET'S GET BACK TO THE **CASTLE OF A THOUSAND ROOMS...**
GROAN! COOL PARTY, BUT I'M BEAT!
I'LL BET! YOU DANCED WITH MINNIE THE WHOLE TIME!

YAWN! I ESTIMATE THERE'S A 54.6% CHANCE I'LL FALL ASLEEP BEFORE REACHING MY BED!
FRUSH
FRUSH

AND WHILE THE CASTLE SLUMBERS...

..SOMEONE GETS READY FOR ACTION, INSIDE...
LET'S GET TO WORK!
...AND OUTSIDE THE CASTLE AS WELL!
LET'S HEAD TO THE CASTLE!
ACTIVATE THE ***INVISIBILITY SHIELD!***
RIGHT AWAY, BOSS!
CLACK

FSS-SSSS-HHH

23

THE NEXT DAY...
MICKEY! WAKE UP!

OH? HUH? 'SUP? A CHALLENGE?
?

NO, DON'T WORRY! BUT... SOMEONE'S WAITING FOR YOU IN THE MAIN HALL!
OH! TEAM MAGMA FIRE!
MICKEY, THE VENERABLE ORMEN SENDS HIS REGARDS AND...

...A PRESENT!

WOW! FIVE DIAMAGIC!

WHY SO GENEROUS, NOBLE ZEFREN?
THE VENERABLE ORMEN THINKS YOU DESERVE THEM FOR THE FRIENDSHIP YOU SHOWED OUR KIND.

AND WHILE WE STILL BELIEVE YOU NO-SCALES SHOULDN'T BE ALLOWED TO USE MAGIC...

...WE WON'T QUESTION ORMEN, THE WISEST OF DRAGONS.
THAT'S RIGHT, BROTHER ZEFREN.

WELL, LET'S ABSORB THEM INTO MY MAGICAL STAFF!
WOOOOOSHH

IT CHANGED AGAIN!

YOU'RE A **LEVEL-6** WIZARD NOW, AND YOUR STAFF REPRESENTS THE NEW POWERS YOU'VE ACQUIRED!

THIS SYMBOL IS FOR THE POWER OF LIGHT—THEN YOU'VE GOT FIRE, CLOUDS...

...AND THIS...HUH? I DUNNO WHAT THAT SYMBOL MEANS!

HMM...IT JUST LOOKS LIKE A **SCRATCH**!
HEY! MINE'S SCRATCHED UP TOO!
SO'S MINE!
MINE TOO!

THIS CAN'T BE A COINCIDENCE!
NO. AND I THINK I KNOW WHAT HAPPENED!

"REMEMBER THE FILES PETE AND THE BEAGLE BOYS WERE CARRYING?"
CLANG

SURE! THEY WOULDN'T ADMIT THEY USED THEM TO BREAK OUT OF JAIL!
THEY WEREN'T LYING. THEY HADN'T USED THEM YET...

...BUT THEY WERE GONNA, TO SCRAPE SOME BITS OFF OUR STAFFS!

I BET THEY DID IT WHEN WE WERE ASLEEP, AFTER THE PARTY!
ACTUALLY, THEY'RE THE ONLY ONES MISSING...

OKAY, BUT...WHAT ARE THEY UP TO?
HMM...I DUNNO. IT'S WEIRD!

THAT'S WEIRD TOO! A-HYUCK! A CLOUD FLYING **INTO THE WIND!** THE PROBABILITY OF THAT HAPPENING IS **ZERO!**

-GASP- IT'S NOT A CLOUD. IT'S A CAMOUFLAGED FLYING SHIP!

HAR-HAR! SEE YA, LOSERS!
IF YOU NEED A HANDYMAN, GIVE US A CALL. OUR FILES ARE...AT YOUR SERVICE! MWAH-HA-HA!

GRRR! THEY WON'T GET AWAY! **STAFF, LENGTHEN!**

GOT ROOM FOR A **PASSENGER?**

SWIIISH

TU-THUMP

GRRR! I'LL TEACH YOU A LESSON, MOUSE!
SWIIISSSS

STOP! I'LL HANDLE THE ***INTRUDERS*** ON MY SHIP!
FOOOSHH
ROKNAR, ***ROAST THEM!***

TUR-AQUOS-SHELL! WATER SHIELD!
FSS-SSS

REMARKABLE! YOUR POWERS HAVE GROWN SINCE THE LAST TIME WE MET...

PHANTOM BLOT?! WEREN'T YOU...?
...IMPRISONED IN ANOTHER DIMENSION? WELL, I'M BACK!

"YOUR MASTER, NEREUS, THOUGHT HE COULD KEEP ME UNDER CONTROL IN THAT DESOLATE LAND...

"BUT HE HAD A LITTLE ACCIDENT...
HELP ME!

"...AND I ESCAPED!
HA-HA! GOOD-BYE, MY OLD ENEMY!

"I WALKED FOR DAYS IN THE SNOW UNTIL I STUMBLED ACROSS AN OLD HOUSE...

"...AND DISCOVERED IT WAS WHERE THE FIRST SUPREME SORCERER USED TO LIVE.
CREEK

"AMONG HIS MUSTY PAPERS, I FOUND A MAP OF THE WAY BACK TO OUR DIMENSION...

"...AND AN ANCIENT SPELL FOR MAKING A SINGLE WISH COME TRUE!"

THAT SPELL REQUIRES THE COMBINED ENERGY OF THE STAFFS OF EVERY WIZARD!

SO THAT'S WHY YOU FILED OFF PIECES OF ALL OUR MAGICAL STAFFS!

THAT'S RIGHT! THOSE FRAGMENTS CONTAIN THE STAFFS' MAGICAL ENERGY...

...AND WILL GRANT ME MY WISH— TO FIND THE CAPITAL OF THE DRAGONS' KINGDOM WHERE THEIR SECRETS ARE HIDDEN!

GASP! THAT'S TERRIBLE! IF PHANTOM BLOT STEALS THE DRAGONS' SECRETS, HE'LL BE INVINCIBLE!

HMM...I GOTTA STOP HIM! WHAT IF...?

SO YOUR WISH IS TO DISCOVER WHERE THE DRAGONS' WISDOM IS KEPT, HUH?

YES! THAT'S PRECISELY WHAT I'M GONNA ASK FOR!
SWHIISH

ARE YOU NUTS? YOU JUST TOLD HIM EXACTLY WHAT TO SAY!
TRUST ME!

I WANT MY SHIP AND ITS CREW TO MATERIALIZE WHERE THE **DRAGONS' WISDOM** IS KEPT!
BZZ-ZZ...

ZA-AAP

HEY! WHAT'S THIS PLACE? WHERE'S THE DRAGONS' KINGDOM?
ZAP

M-MASTER...THIS IS THE VENERABLE ORMEN'S CAVE!
HE'S THE **CUSTODIAN OF THE DRAGONS' WISDOM**...JUST LIKE YOU ASKED!

OF COURSE, IF YOU'D WISHED TO FIND THE **LIBRARY** OF THE DRAGONS' KINGDOM, YOU COULD'VE RANSACKED IT...

...WHEREAS I DON'T THINK ORMEN'S GONNA TELL YOU HIS MAGICAL SECRETS!
HEH-HEH! WELL DONE, MICKEY!

YOU CAN ALWAYS TRY TO CONVINCE HIM!
ROAAAR! WHO DARES DISTURB MY REST?

ARGH! LET'S GET AWAY FROM HERE!
VRRRRRL

GOOD-BYE, PHANTOM BLOT! AND REMEMBER—BE CAREFUL WHAT YOU WISH FOR!

GOTCHA!
PAF

GRRR! THIS ISN'T OVER! I'LL BE BACK!

ONCE AGAIN, YOU'VE PROVED YOU'RE CUNNING AND WISE, MICKEY.

YOU MUST BE PART DRAGON! HEH-HEH!

AND I'M WISE ENOUGH TO KNOW IT'S BETTER TO HAVE AN ***UMBRELLA*** WHEN IT'S SNOWING.
HEH-HEH!
ANOTHER ADVENTURE IS OVER, AND THE TOURNAMENT'S ABOUT TO END... BUT THERE'S **ONE LAST CHALLENGE** TO OVERCOME!
THE END

Wizards of Mickey

Wizards of Mickey
Walt Disney
Chapter 10
The Supreme Sorcerer

IT WAS THE TIME OF LEGENDS, OF WIZARDS AND HEROES...
AND SPEAKING OF HEROES, MEET THE **WIZARDS OF MICKEY**!
DONALD: AN UNLUCKY WIZARD. HE CAN ONLY CAST DELAYED-ACTION SPELLS.
MICKEY: WIZARD FROM THE VILLAGE OF MICELAND. HIS MASTER, NEREUS, IS TRAPPED IN ANOTHER DIMENSION.
GOOFY: FATED TO BE A WIZARD...BUT HE'D RATHER DO SOMETHING ELSE.
FAFNIR: A BABY DRAGON.
PHANTOM BLOT: HE WANTS TO BECOME THE SUPREME SORCERER. HE COMMANDS THE BLACK PHANTOMS TEAM—PETE AND THE BEAGLE BOYS.
THE GREAT CROWN: GIVES THE WEARER ULTIMATE POWER! IT CAN ONLY BE REBUILT BY THE WIZARD WHO WINS ALL THE DIAMAGIC CRYSTALS IN THE **GRAND SORCERERS TOURNAMENT**.
TOURNAMENT RULES
*TEAMS OF THREE WIZARDS COMPETE IN MAGICAL CHALLENGES.
*THE CHALLENGES TAKE PLACE IN THE CASTLES MARKED ON THE OFFICIAL MAP.
*FOR EVERY CHALLENGE, EACH TEAM MUST STAKE THEIR DIAMAGIC.
*THE WINNER TAKES THE OPPONENT'S DIAMAGIC.
*THOSE LEFT WITHOUT A DIAMAGIC CRYSTAL ARE DISQUALIFIED.

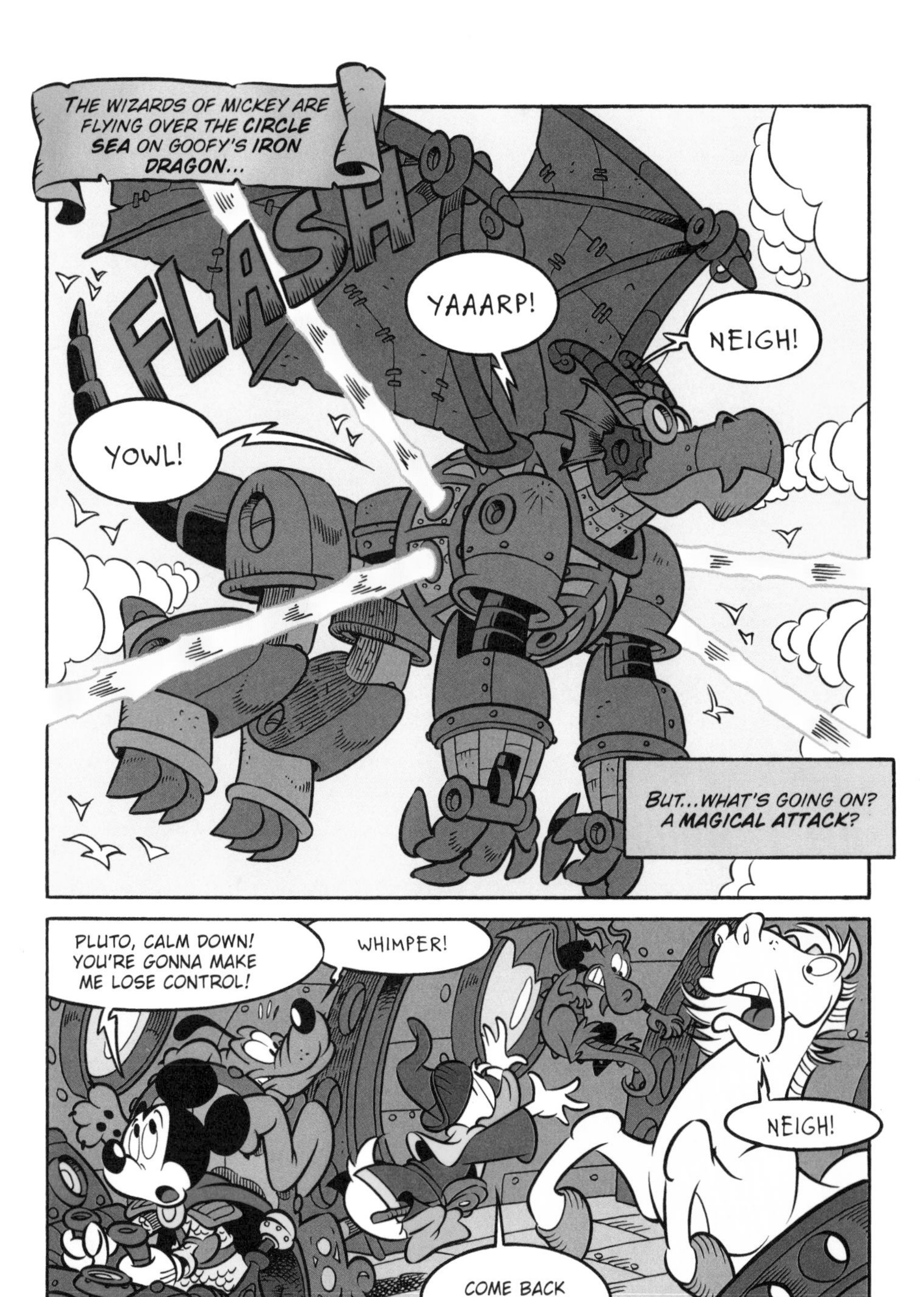
THE WIZARDS OF MICKEY ARE FLYING OVER THE CIRCLE SEA ON GOOFY'S IRON DRAGON...
FLASH
YAAARP!
NEIGH!
YOWL!
BUT...WHAT'S GOING ON? A MAGICAL ATTACK?
PLUTO, CALM DOWN! YOU'RE GONNA MAKE ME LOSE CONTROL!
WHIMPER!
NEIGH!
COME BACK HERE, FAFNIR!

NOT AN ATTACK! IT WAS A MAGNESIUM FLASH!
A-HYUCK! GUESS OUR FRIENDS DON'T LIKE BEING PHOTO-GRAPHED!

HMPH! 'COURSE NOT. THIS THING IS BLINDING!
SWIIIIISS

GOOFY! WHAT WEIRD JOB HAVE YOU COME UP WITH NOW?

PHOTOGRAPHY! IT'S LIKE PAINTING, BUT QUICKER...

48

...SO I CAN DOCUMENT THE REST OF THE TOURNAMENT!
RELAX! COUGH! IT'S NOT A "MAKE THE MOST SMOKE" CONTEST!
GRRR...

HEH-HEH! GOOFY'S FULL OF SURPRISES...
Mickey, can you hear me?

I CAN HEAR YOU JUST FINE! 'SUP?
HUH?
HMM?

UMM...ACTUALLY, WE DIDN'T SAY A WORD.

HMM...BUT I'M SURE I HEARD SOMETHING...

AHA! I WAS RIGHT!
Mickey! Mickey!

YOU MAKING FUN OF ME. OR WHAT?
I DUNNO WHAT YOU'RE ON ABOUT...ANYWAY, LOOK OUTSIDE!

IT'S *TURBO*, THE TOURNAMENT MESSENGER!

HE MUST BE BRINGING US THE UPDATED *MAP* OF THE CASTLES WHERE THE CHALLENGES WILL BE HELD. LET HIM IN!

A-HYUCK! I WANNA SNAP A PICTURE OF HIM!

NO, WAIT... GULP!
FLASH

GLUB!

OUCH!
SBAM

...
GASP! GOOFY, TAKE THE CONTROLS WHILE I HELP HIM.
AND PUT THAT STUPID THING **AWAY!**
GROAN!
SWIIISSS

WH-WHERE AM I...? OH, YES! HERE'S THE NEW MAP.

GET TO THE LOCATION OF THE NEW CHALLENGE AS QUICKLY AS YOU CAN!

HMM...LOOKS LIKE ALL THE TEAMS HAVE TO GATHER IN THE **SAME CASTLE!**
FANGS CASTLE

WEIRD! USUALLY, THERE ARE MANY CHALLENGES ALL AT ONCE IN DIFFERENT CASTLES.
WELL, LET'S SET OUR COURSE AND CHECK IT OUT.

Careful, Mickey! Do not rush!
?!
I HEARD RIGHT! SOMEONE CALLED ME, BUT... THE VOICE CAME FROM THE MEDALOPHONE.
I DON'T GET IT! ONLY MASTER NEREUS EVER USED IT TO CONTACT ME...
"BUT HE STOPPED AFTER...
Mickey, if you are listening to this recording, it means I am no longer in this dimension...
"AND ACCORDING TO PHANTOM BLOT, MY MASTER FELL INTO A TRAP..."
HA-HA-HA!
IT'S A REAL MYSTER— URGH! WH-WHAT'S HAPPENING?
I TURNED THE BLASTERS ON. HOLD TIGHT!

WOOOOOSSH

SO AFTER A **SUPER-FAST** JOURNEY...
HERE WE ARE! **FANGS CASTLE!**

I WANNA TAKE A PICTURE FROM ABOVE!
HEY! DON'T LEAVE THE CONTROLS!

LOOK...YOU CAN SEE WIZARDS FIGHTING!

A-HYUCK! NEVER SEEN SO MANY CHALLENGES AT ONCE!
RAIN OF ROCKS!
THORNY VINES!

"EVEN THOSE FRIENDLY WIZARD-COOKS ARE FIGHTING TOOTH AND NAIL."
AND THEY'RE SO AGGRESSIVE!
SAUSAGE LASSO!

"AND LOOK AT DAISY! SHE'S ON *FIRE*!"
SCORCHING FLAMES!

SOMETHING'S NOT RIGHT! WE'D BETTER INVESTIGATE BEFORE JOINING THE OTHERS.

LET'S LAND OUTSIDE THE CASTLE WALLS AND SNEAK IN!
FSSSSSSS

PLUTO, YOU CAN'T LOOK FOR MOLES NOW!
SNIFF, SNIFF!

NOT MOLES! HE FOUND A ***WEASEL GOBLIN***!
WOOF!

NOT JUST ONE! THERE'S A WHOLE ARMY!
YEEEK! YEEEK!

PLUTO, TRANSFORM!
ROOOAR!

VOOOSSH

HEY, NOT SO FAST! MY PHOTO WILL BE BLURRY!
YEEEEK!

WHY DON'CHA PHOTOGRAPH THIS...BEFORE I HIT YOU ON THE HEAD WITH IT?

HAR-HAR! WELCOME, WIZARDS OF MICKEY!
WE WERE EXPECTING YOU!

BET YOU **CAN'T WAIT** TO CHALLENGE ME TO A DUEL, HUH?

TSK! **NO WAY!** CHEATERS LIKE YOU SHOULDN'T EVEN BE ADMITTED TO THE TOURNAMENT!
HUH?

UMM...PETE, THESE GUYS DON'T SEEM TO HAVE ANY INTENTION OF FIGHTING.

YEAH! HMM...I DON'T GET IT! LOOKS LIKE THE **HOSTILITY SPELL** DIDN'T WORK ON THEM.

SPELL?! THAT MEANS THE OTHER WIZARDS ARE BEING SO VIOLENT 'COS OF MAGIC!
WHOOPS! I SAID TOO MUCH.

WELL, YOU'RE GONNA FIGHT, WHETHER YOU LIKE IT OR NOT, MOUSE!
TUMP

NO! YOU'LL HAVE TO DEAL WITH ME FIRST!
FOOOSH

YOU AND PHANTOM BLOT USED ME FOR YOUR PLAN! YOU'RE GONNA PAY FOR THAT!

I'LL SEND YOU TO THE HIGHEST PEAK OF THE IMPASSABLE MOUNTAINS!
FOOOOOSH
ARGH!
I GOTCHA, FAFNIR!

THIS ISN'T OVER, MOUUUUUUUSE...

GREAT JOB! NOW CALM DOWN AND TELL US WHAT HAPPENED!

THOSE SCOUNDRELS CAPTURED AND HYPNOTIZED ME! SO FOLLOWING THEIR ORDERS, EVERY TIME I DELIVERED A MAP...

"...I CAST THE HOSTILITY SPELL ON THE WIZARDS."
ZOT

BUT WHY NOT ON US?
BECAUSE OF THE FLASH FROM GOOFY'S CAMERA.

"IT BLINDED ME! SO I HIT THE WALL, AND..."
SBAM
FLASH

...IT BROKE THE HYPNOSIS!
HEH-HEH! I WON'T SAY YOUR PHOTOS ARE USELESS ANYMORE.

AT FIRST, I COULDN'T REMEMBER WHAT HAPPENED...BUT THEN I DID! AND I WENT LOOKING FOR PETE TO TEACH HIM A LESSON!

I STILL DON'T GET PETE'S PLAN. WHY MAKE THE WIZARDS SO AGGRESSIVE?

?!
To make them fight one another until they are exhausted! Then, he'll attack once they are too weak to defend themselves!

MASTER NEREUS?! I-IS THAT YOU?

So he can snatch all the Diamagic at once! You must stop him... Bzzzt...

WE LOST CONTACT! WELL, I'LL SOLVE THIS MYSTERY LATER!

NOW, LET'S RUN TO THE CASTLE! WE GOTTA STOP PHANTOM BLOT!

THUMP

TSK! TELLING PETE AND THE BEAGLE BOYS THE PLAN WAS A MISTAKE.

NEVER SEND NO-SCALES TO DO A DRAGON'S JOB!
FOOSSHH
WACK!

SGNAC

YOU INSOLENT BABY! I'LL TEACH YOU THAT DRAGONS AREN'T FIREPROOF EITHER!

FOOSSH

MICKEY, GET TO THE CASTLE! I'LL HANDLE THE DRAGON!
OUCH!
FSSS

TIME TO TRY MY IRON DRAGON'S ***BATTLE SETTING***!
GROOOARR

RAAAWR!
FIREPROOF WING-SHIELD!
LET'S GET INSIDE!
HOW'RE WE GONNA STOP PHANTOM BLOT?
I DUNNO! BREAKING THE HOSTILITY SPELL WOULD BE USELESS...

"PHANTOM BLOT HAS **ALREADY ACHIEVED** HIS GOAL!"
PANT, PANT!
I DON'T EVEN HAVE THE STRENGTH FOR A **SNACK**!

IT'S TIME! IN ACCORDANCE WITH THE TOURNAMENT'S RULES, I ***CHALLENGE*** YOU!

AND SINCE YOU'RE TOO TIRED TO FIGHT BACK, A ***PARALYSIS SPELL*** IS ENOUGH TO DEFEAT YOU ALL.

HA-HA! I HAVEN'T TURNED ANYONE TO STONE SINCE MY ATTACK ON MOON-LAND KINGDOM. WHAT FUN!
I-IT WAS YOU...YOU ***DESTROYED*** MY KINGDOM...

NOW THAT YOU'RE DEFEATED, I'M TAKING YOUR *DIAMAGIC*... ALL ACCORDING TO THE RULES!

WACK! HE'S ABOUT TO UNITE ALL THE MAGICAL CRYSTALS. HE'S GONNA *REBUILD* THE SUPREME SORCERER'S CROWN!

I WAS WAITING FOR YOU, MICKEY! I ACCEPT YOUR CHALLENGE... WHICH I WILL WIN *RIGHT NOW!*
VOOOOOSH
NO WAY! PROTECTIVE WALL!
CRIC CRIC CRAC

RAG-FLASH-ZAAAAP! PIERCING LIGHTNING BOLT!

CRAAK
URGH!

GULP! WE'RE ALL GONNA END UP *PLUCKED!*

MEANWHILE...
BURN, YOU FAKE DRAGON!

PANT! I'M NEVER GONNA DEFEAT ROKNAR USING THE SAME WEAPONS AS HIM!

LET'S SEE HOW HE FARES AGAINST MY IRON DRAGON...
TLAC

...in Firefighter Mode!
SPROOSSSH

ARGH! GLUB! FIREFIGHTING FOAM...GLUB!

I CAN'T BREATHE FIRE ANYMORE! NOOOO!

WOO-HOO! HE'S RUNNING AWAY!
ROKNAR—0, IRON DRAGON—1!

DID YOU SEE THAT, GUYS...? GULP!

"A-HYUCK! POOR MICKEY! I WOULDN'T WANNA BE IN HIS SHOES!"
ZOT
ZOT
ZOT

IT'S OVER, MOUSE! YOU'RE DEFEATED... AND YOUR DIAMAGIC WILL BE MINE!

OH NO! IT'S TOO SOON! IF ONLY I HAD MORE TIME...

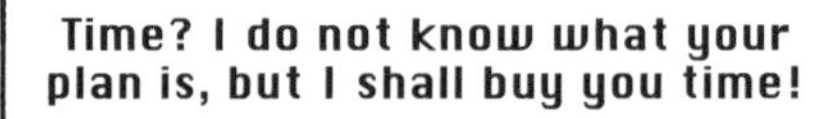
Time? I do not know what your plan is, but I shall buy you time!

HUH? WHAT...?

HELLO, ***OLD ENEMY***! YOU WERE NOT EXPECTING TO SEE ME AGAIN, I PRESUME.

MASTER NEREUS?!
HOW CAN IT BE? LAST TIME I SAW YOU, YOU WERE...
...***TRAPPED*** IN THE FROZEN LAKE WHERE YOU ***ABANDONED ME***? INDEED! I THOUGHT THERE WAS NO WAY OUT EITHER...
"BUT I HAD AN IDEA! I TRANSFORMED INTO A ***SPECK OF DUST***...
"...SO I COULD BREAK FREE AND FOLLOW YOU, CARRIED BY THE WIND!"

"I LANDED ON YOUR MEDALLION...
"...WHERE I HID WHILE I *REGAINED* MY STRENGTH.
"WHEN YOU RETURNED TO OUR DIMENSION, YOU TOOK ME WITH YOU..."
SO IN THE END, YOU WERE THE ONE WHO SAVED ME!
GRRR! EVEN BETTER...
...YOU CAME BACK JUST IN TIME TO SEE ME *DEFEAT* YOUR APPRENTICE...AND BE CROWNED *SUPREME SORCERER*!

HERE WE GO! HE HIT MY STAFF WITH THE SPELL TO ABSORB THE DIAMAGIC. AND IF MY CALCULATIONS WERE RIGHT...
VOOSSH

YES! THE **REFLECTION SPELL** WORKED!
ZZAAP

WHAT? **THAT'S IMPOSSIBLE!** I DIDN'T SEE YOU CAST ANY SPELL!

THAT'S 'COS I DIDN'T! DONALD DID, AND SINCE HIS SPELLS ALWAYS RUN LATE...

...YOU TRIED TO ABSORB MY DIAMAGIC RIGHT WHEN THE **REFLECTION SPELL** ACTIVATED!
VOOSSH
SO INSTEAD OF YOUR STAFF ABSORBING MY DIAMAGIC, **MINE** IS ABSORBING **YOURS**!

YOU KNOW WHAT THAT MEANS? NOW THAT I'VE GOT ALL THE DIAMAGIC...

...I CAN RESTORE THE GREAT CROWN!

YOUR REIGN OF EVIL IS OVER! GO AWAY! VANISH INTO THE SHADOWS!
NOOO!

AAAAARGH!

WH-WHAT HAPPENED?
HE BECAME A **SHADOW**, LIKE YOU ORDERED!

YOU ARE THE **SUPREME SORCERER** NOW! YOU'VE BEEN GIVEN GREAT POWER...USE IT **WISELY**!

SO AFTER FREEING THE OTHER WIZARDS FROM THE PARALYSIS SPELL, IT'S TIME TO **CELEBRATE**!
A-HYUCK! SAY **CHEESE**! TIME FOR A PHOTO!
HOORAY FOR MICKEY!
HOORAY FOR THE SUPREME SORCERER!
THE FIRST **WIZARDS OF MICKEY** SAGA IS OVER! NOW TURN THE PAGE FOR...

Wizards of Mickey

Coming Soon
Wizards of Mickey II
The Dark Age

Bonus Content

From the pages of *Topolino*, a world famous Italian comic anthology featuring works from Disney, *Wizards of Mickey* stands out as one of the most iconic Disney comics.

It is our pleasure to share with you here some of the magazine artwork from those original issues on the following pages.

Enjoy!

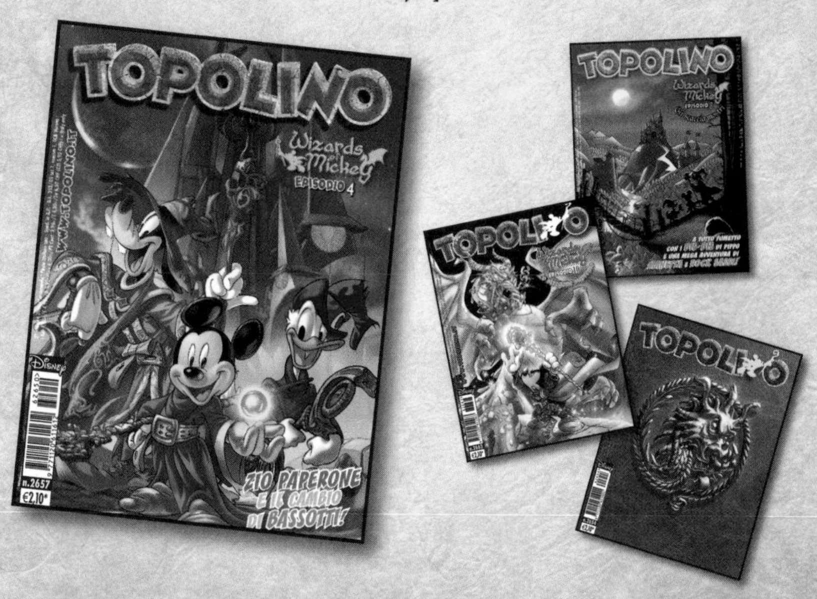

SEE YOU IN VOLUME 2!

Wizards of Mickey

Wizards of Mickey 1

This book is a work of fiction. Names, characters, places, and incidents are the product of the author's imagination or are used fictitiously. Any resemblance to actual events, locales, or persons, living or dead, is coincidental.

JY
150 West 30th Street, 19th Floor
New York, NY 10001

Visit us at jyforkids.com
facebook.com/jyforkids
twitter.com/jyforkids
jyforkids.tumblr.com
instagram.com/jyforkids

First JY Edition: November 2020

JY is an imprint of Yen Press, LLC.
The JY name and logo are trademarks of Yen Press, LLC.

The publisher is not responsible for websites (or their content) that are not owned by the publisher.

Library of Congress Control Number: 2020944890

ISBNs: 978-1-9753-1903-8 (paperback)
978-1-9753-1904-5 (ebook)

10 9 8 7 6 5 4 3 2

LSC-C

Printed in the United States of America

Cover Art by Marco Ghiglione
with colors by Massimo Rocca

Translation by Linda Ghio and
Stephanie Dagg at Editing Zone
Lettering by Katie Blakeslee

THE GRAND TOURNAMENT
Story by Stefano Ambrosio
Art by Lorenzo Pastrovicchio

THE DOLMEN SWAMP
Story by Stefano Ambrosio
Art by Marco Gervaslo

THE SECRET OF THE GREAT CROWN
Story by Stefano Ambrosio
Art by Marco Palazzi

MOON DIAMOND
Story by Stefano Ambrosio
Art by Alessandro Perina

THE WELL OF DRAGONS
Story by Stefano Ambrosio
Art by Marco Mazzarello

WITCHES IN THE PALACE
Story by Stefano Ambrosio
Art by Vitale Mangiatordi

THE IRON DRAGON
Story by Stefano Ambrosio
Art by Lorenzo Pastrovicchio

THE MONSTER HUNTERS
Story by Stefano Ambrosio
Art by Alessandro Pastrovicchio

THE RETURN OF PHANTOM BLOT
Story by Stefano Ambrosio
Art by Marco Gervasio

THE SUPREME SORCERER
Story by Stefano Ambrosio
Art by Marco Palazzi